BOOKS BY ANTHONY BURGESS
(in the order in which they were written)

NOVELS
A Vision of Battlements
The Long Day Wanes
The Right to an Answer
The Doctor Is Sick
Devil of a State
A Clockwork Orange
The Wanting Seed
Honey for the Bears
Nothing Like the Sun
Tremor of Intent
Enderby

NONFICTION
Re Joyce
The Novel Now
Urgent Copy

The Eve

of Saint Venus

ANTHONY BURGESS

Illustrated by Edward Pagram

W · W · Norton & Company · Inc · NEW YORK

First published as a Norton paperback 1979.

W. W. Norton & Company, Inc., also publishes *The Norton Anthology of English Literature,* edited by M. H. Abrams et al; *The Norton Anthology of Poetry,* edited by Arthur M. Eastman et al; *World Masterpieces,* edited by Maynard Mack et al; *The Norton Reader,* edited by Arthur M. Eastman et al; *The Norton Facisimile of the First Folio of Shakespeare,* prepared by Charlton Hinman; *The Norton Anthology of Modern Poetry,* edited by Richard Ellmann and Robert O'Clair; *The Norton Anthology of Short Fiction,* edited by R. V. Cassill; and the *Norton Critical Editions.*

The Library of Congress cataloged the first printing of this title as follows:

Burgess, Anthony, 1917-
The eve of Saint Venus [by] Anthony Burgess. Illustrated by
Edward Pagram. [1st American ed.] New York, Norton
[1970, c 1964]

1. Title.
PZ4.B953 Ev   1970   823'.9'14   79-108328
[PR6052.U638]
ISBN   0-393-08602-X
ISBN   0-393-00915-7 pbk.

1 2 3 4 5 6 7 8 9 0

To

BERNARD B. BROWN, B.A.

Lieut-Commander, R.N.R.

Foreword to the American Edition

I WROTE this libellum or opusculum or *jeu d'esprit* in, I think, 1950 but did not publish it in England until the fall of 1964. There were various reasons for the long gap between the striking of the scintilla and entrusting it to the cupped hands of publication. The reasons had mainly to do with the book's slightness, lack of earnestness, blindness to the spirit of social commitment. With so many didactic heavyweights on the publishers' lists, it was felt that it would be too easily bruised or, worse, jostled into the kennel and ignored. With a sufficient number of, well, welterweights of my own to protect it by 1964, it was considered safe to bring it out in that year. British critics did not ignore it, but some of them looked in it for more than is there, and some of them for less.

The five years between British and American publication have to be explained differently. It takes time to establish an English novelist in the United States, and this is considered to be a very "English" book. The term can be taken disparagingly. *The Eve of Saint Venus*—which is, incidentally, the way I translate *Pervigilium Veneris,* the name of the Latin hymn to the goddess which appears, straight or garbled, in the later part of the book —is whimsical, like *Peter Pan* (which was written by a Scotsman), and it depends for its effects largely on an understanding of the insular and conservative English character, especially as

1

manifested in a silly, ingrown, mainly non-existent rural aristocracy. It is English also in a technical, dramaturgical, sense. As the *commedia dell' arte* is Italian, so the *commedia dell'* Aldwych is, or was, English. For many years at the Aldwych Theatre in London, a very successful genre of farcical comedy was presented, skilful if mechanical, with characters as stylised, and plots as vacuously ingenious, as any in Plautus or Terence. There were mild marital misunderstandings, mirrored by tiffs in the merely betrothed state, there were people found in the wrong bedrooms, there was often multiple transvestism, incidental burglary, money bet on the wrong horses. Among the characters were the monocled "silly ass" (a Bertie Wooster unredeemed by any Jeeves), the boneheaded goldhearted country squire in plus-fours, the pert and resourceful servant, the grim but reliable châtelaine, the sweet, guileless young lovers, the comic Anglican clergyman.

My aim was to write a novella constructed rather like one of the old Aldwych farces, with classical unity of time and setting, an ageless "county" atmosphere, a cast of stock characters. One of the characters is not, in fact, taken from stock—I mean Julia Webb, the lesbian journalist. But all the others derive from the traditional British comedy which, in one form or another, has proved unkillable. Banish it from the stage and it turns up on the screen; banish it from the screen—in favour of miniskirts and Cockney abortions—and it turns up on television. Having given myself this stock cast, I attempted to impose two rather highbrow disciplines which would never have been allowed in the Aldwych. The characters had to act in the framework of an ancient story recounted by Burton in *The Anatomy of Melancholy* (that of the young man who, on the eve of his wedding, places the ring on the finger of a statue of Venus and finds the goddess herself pre-empting the marriage bed); they had to speak a somewhat artificial "literary" prose which was meant to be a parody of the poetic drama which had revived in

2

England in the late 'forties—more the language of Christopher Fry than of T. S. Eliot, though Old Possum lurks there too.

As the story was first drafted in the grey days of the British Welfare State, I felt compelled to make my obligatory chuckle-headed old baronet a very nostalgic Tory, full of reminiscences of great meals and fine wines—Falstaffian in a sense, and indeed carrying a Shakespearean association in his very name. He is Sir Benjamin Drayton. Benjamin Jonson and Michael Drayton were present at Shakespeare's last, and lethal, supper. The old nurse is meant to have elements of Juliet's Nurse in her. And, of course, the very theme of the goddess Venus pursuing a young, not very bright, mortal man is a Shakespearean one. All these aspects were appropriate to the year 1964 and Shakespeare's quater-centenary. And I have made two alterations to the original text which will enable the reader to place the action of the book in 1964, or certainly the early 'sixties.

I do not apologise for the humility of my purpose, which was, and still is, to entertain. The deeper theme—which is about the importance of physical love—must seem trite coming from a middleaged writer, though it is invariably fresh and surprising in a haired and naked juvenile. As for the Englishry, which I might have had to apologise for before Englishry became acceptable, even fleetingly modish, in the United States, I no longer have much sympathy with it. I become every day more and more one quarter Irish; I am married to an Italian contessa of revolutionary leanings; I live on a Catholic Semitic Island. But the story is, I think, a fair and plausible representation of how certain English types might behave if ever Venus really did, fulfilling the prophecy of the Purcell song, make her dwelling on that other island and forsake her Cyprian groves.

A. B.

Lija, Malta

3

THE EVE OF SAINT VENUS

This is based on a tale told by Burton (*Anatomy of Melancholy*: Pt. 3, Sec. 2, Mem. I, Subs. I) which he got from Florilegus, ad annum 1058, "an honest historian of our nation, because he telleth it so confidently, as a thing in those days talked of all over Europe".

I

"CLUSTERFIST. Slipshop demisemiwit." Sir Benjamin Drayton's swearing was always too literary to be really offensive. "Decerebrated clodpoles, that's all we have, that's all we have. Sense? Sense, you garboil, you ugly lusk, you unsavoury mound of droppings, sense? Have you no sense? Those things," said Sir Benjamin, "are priceless. You tripes, lights, frowsty chitterling. Priceless, do you hear? You chuffcat. Must I be foiled, fooled, fouled at every turn by wanton smashers and deliberate defilers? Goths, the Goths are coming. The Vandals are hunting me down. Give me patience."

Spatchcock, the maid, was an ugly girl but a girl of spirit, well able to stand up for herself, reasonable withal in the face of her master's ranting. "I only touched it, sir," she said. "It came to pieces like. It must have got damaged on the way, sir, in transit like. That shaking in the van can't have done them much good, sir, or it wouldn't have dropped off like."

"Wouldn't have dropped off like," mocked Sir Benjamin, sneering. "What is this? What are you in real life? What archconspiracy of iconoclasts put you on to me? What, you effluvium, you miasmal fog, is the enemy paying you? We needs must loathe the highest when we see it.

That's the motto of your organisation, isn't it?"

"I don't know what you mean," said Spatchcock, "sir."

"I don't know what you mean," mocked Sir Benjamin, "sir." "I mean this, you sediment, you lees, you leavings, you flasket of unwholesome guts. Be consistent about it. Consume a first folio, leaf by leaf, in the lavatory. Daub moustaches, with a dirty finger, on a Da Vinci. Have a good time, go the whole hog, smash my statues."

"I was only having a look at them," sulked Spatchcock.

"A look at them," echoed Sir Benjamin. "Who told you to have a look at them? That face is lethal. Weren't you ever told that? If they weren't stone already they would have been petrified. Out of my sight, you Medusa. I'll pound you, pound you. My patience is well-known. Give it air."

"If I didn't know my place," said Spatchcock, "I'd say that you was a foul old fustilugs and a mannerless old cod. And what's more, I'd tell you what to do with them. If I didn't know my place, I'd wish St Anthony's fire and the quinance and the flux on your nasty old carcase for taking advantage of a girl's lack of education. But I know my place, so I'll say nothing." And she went out, head up, not without dignity.

Sir Benjamin breathed heavily, looking up at the portrait of the first baronet, Sir Edward Bulwer Drayton, a Liberal honoured in the Gladstone ministry of 1868-74. Sir Edward looked down in chop-fed sternness. Would he have put up with it? Sir Benjamin decided that he would not have worried overmuch. A pious Utilitarian who had once inveighed against Ruskin in a public lecture, who had disfigured this rural landscape with chimneys that puffed out, like huge cigars, the many noughts of his fortune, he had had no love of the arts, believing that pushpin was *better* than poetry. Had not this Gothic mansion been considered, even by the standards of his day, hideous? Perhaps, in these nineteen-sixties, it was appreciated as much as it ever had been or would be: its cupolas, steeples, architraves were slammed on to a shambling limping monster that, in its gracelessness, people could feel sorry for. The motherly English countryside caressed the ugly beast, the soft air licked the soft local stone like a bear-cub. England could assimilate anything.

"Is anything wrong, Ben?" asked Lady Drayton. She had been writing, had vaguely noticed noise. Twenty years younger than her husband, a plumply handsome county lady, she looked up. Sir Benjamin was sarcastic; he said:

"No, no, nothing's wrong at all. Except that that crawling lump of Derbyshire neck, that unpricked boil that you call a maid (maid, indeed) has broken a finger off."

"Oh," said Lady Drayton, still vague. "And does it hurt, dear?"

"Does it hurt?" said Sir Benjamin. "It hurts like hell. I'd rather lose one of my own than see those statues suffer. They're priceless, priceless. When you think of the trouble my brother had shipping them all the way from Syracuse or wherever it was, when you think of the heartburn I've had while British Railways has been playing dice with them all the way from the docks, when you think of what it means to me to have the whole set of them, all those gods and goddesses, the spoils of Greece, the grace and gold of the ancient world, can you honestly say that you think my language immoderate?"

"You can mend it, dear," said Lady Drayton. "No damage is irreparable. Besides, I never thought that gods had to have fingers. Surely Venus is completely without arms? Diana, as a child, you remember, had a book with a picture of Venus without arms, and I always told her to keep it in mind when she felt like biting her nails."

"My Venus," said Sir Benjamin, "has arms. So have the

9

others. But for how long now depends on your maid."

"Don't worry, dear," said Lady Drayton. "Your statues will have to submit to greater indignities. The birds just love our garden."

"They should be inside," said Sir Benjamin. "When can I move them indoors?"

"There isn't room," said Lady Drayton. "Not at the moment, anyway. What with guests and presents, there won't be a cubic inch to spare, and anyway it would be rather embarrassing to have all that nakedness adding more heat to the house. And you know old Major ffoulkes: he's very shortsighted and will talk to anyone. I don't want him to think that any of our other guests are offering him dumb insolence."

"Well," said Sir Benjamin, "it's a damned nuisance. But it's never been first things first, never. They arranged old Bannerman's funeral, you may remember, on the day of the Grand National."

"You know," said Lady Drayton, pursuing her own thoughts, "I can hardly believe it. Just fancy tomorrow being Diana's wedding-day. It only seems last week that she was presented to me, like some new publication wet from the press, the proofs of a laborious novel. A little rose-coloured bundle with a puling Churchillian face. You could see even then that she was going to be pretty."

"All children," pronounced Sir Benjamin, "look like monkeys. And ugly monkeys at that. I can never understand why more boys aren't christened Simeon."

"And here she is," said Lady Drayton, "at a station that used to be so far away in the future as almost to be mythical. This is the terminus as far as I'm concerned. Her first tooth, her first sentence, her first day away at school, her first long dress, and now her first marriage."

"How many did you have in mind?" asked Sir Benjamin.

"Well," said Lady Drayton, "it doesn't do to brood. Work, work is the thing. There's plenty to do. I've just been writing out the menu. It's in French, of course a rather impressionistic French, but I think it will be sufficiently unintelligible. My genders are shaky, but they don't have to eat the genders."

"You might as well," said Sir Benjamin, "have done it in English." He started to read it through, first having clamped spectacles on his rocky bushy face, grunting.

"Puritanism," said Lady Drayton. "People are scared of nakedness. They'll be scared of those statues of yours. The English take their pleasures sadly. They like to approach food through a sort of crossword puzzle."

"Food," said Sir Benjamin, nodding. "Food. I always think weddings should be all eating. I seem to remember that ours was a positive orgy. There were, you remember, acres of red meat spitting in the ovens, hissing and singing to a summer of incredible richness, with a fat sap of gravy. Turkeys there were, and capons and woodcock and stubblegeese—a whole roasted aviary. And whole hams, pink as innocence. And all the junkets and flummeries and syllabubs and ice-puddings, sharp as a dentist's probe. What a day that was. And think of the wine, too. Rivers of cold sun from all the provinces that the sun washes. Names like a roll of heroes: Cérons and Barsac, Loupiac, Moulis, Madiran, Blanquette de Limoux, Jurançon, Fleurie, Montrachet, Cumiéres, Armagnac. . . . We'll never see anything like that again. The past is dead, and all that was good is buried with it. And here's this thick horrible door of the present with its tantalising keyhole. You can press your eye or your ear to it, but you can't turn either into a key. The past goes on inside, that perpetual party, becoming wilder and wilder, but there's no admittance."

11

"Ben," said Lady Drayton, "you're getting morbid. You must give up claret with luncheon."

"I am not getting morbid," said Sir Benjamin. "I'm merely stating a truth. Things were better in the past."

"We've been hearing that all week from the Opposition," said a voice. "Forgive me." A personable young man stood by the door. "I heard voices and there was nobody about and the door was open. I just walked in."

"Oh," said Lady Drayton, "hallo, Mr Crowther-Mason. Do come in. It's good to see you. You're here sooner than we expected—too late for tea and a little too soon for cocktails, but very welcome. Was the train early?"

"That," said Sir Benjamin, "is a ridiculous notion."

"I very much doubt it," said Crowther-Mason, more politely. "The tremulous bridegroom gave me a lift in his car. I say 'tremulous' advisedly. I never saw such driving. He traced a sort of fever chart all the way from town. Talk about nerves. Why does marriage take people that way? Is freedom something so valuable that people tremble at the thought of losing it? I shouldn't have thought so."

"You should know all about its price, if not its value," said Sir Benjamin nastily. "You politicians regard it as a saleable commodity."

"Now, Ben," reproved Lady Drayton. "Mr Crowther-Mason's here as a guest, as Ambrose's best man. He wants to forget politics."

"He certainly does," said Sir Benjamin. "It's a dirty business, dirty. I don't trust any of them. They're all grubby. And those who believe in a nice clean healthy future with bathrooms for all and privacy for no one, those are by far the grubbiest."

"Well, sir," said Crowther-Mason, "don't look at me like that. My collar was clean this morning, but what can you expect from an open coupé?"

At this moment Spatchcock returned. Lady Drayton said, "Mr Crowther-Mason's come, Spatchcock. Get somebody to take his case up, will you?"

"Somebody else has come too, my lady," said Spatchcock. "A man outside, carrying on something awful. He won't give no name, but he says he's one of the guests."

"You, is it, you?" said Sir Benjamin. He advanced on Spatchcock with stiff held-out threatening arms. "That iconoclastic face is going to haunt me. Why can't you keep it out of my sight? Why can't you hide it with the dust and blackbeetles and a ghastly crime I was charitably trying to forget?"

Spatchcock turned on him. "I've got to come in, haven't I?" she said. "I've got to say if there's someone at the door, haven't I? It's my job. It's what I get paid for, and you can't stop me, so there."

"What sort of man is it?" asked Lady Drayton.

"Drunk, my lady," said Spatchcock, "and cursing something shocking."

"It's your brother, Ben," said Lady Drayton. "You'd better drag him up to his room and don't forget to lock the door. You know what happened last time."

"People are so narrow-minded nowadays," said Sir Benjamin. "And, besides, he didn't do any harm. You can see much worse in a public art gallery."

"Anyway," said Lady Drayton, "lock that door, and make sure he's properly equipped."

"He brings his own corkscrew," said Sir Benjamin. "Come on, you losel," he said to Spatchcock, "you privy calligrapher, you. You can carry his bottles. I'll carry him." And he went out, rumbling.

"If," said Spatchcock, "I didn't know my place, I'd say that it's just common ignorance, that's all. Gentry you call yourselves. Well, if that's the way gentry behaves I'd as

"Gentry you call yourselves."

14

soon be on a canal barge. I has my self-respect, same as anyone else."

"Thank you, Spatchcock," said Lady Drayton. "That
will do very well."

"It's not you, my lady," said Spatchcock. "You know I
has every respect. It's him," she said, pointing with her
thumb. Then she went out.

"Servants are a problem, aren't they?" said Crowther-
Mason politely.

"I'm afraid my brother-in-law's rather a problem, too,"
said Lady Drayton. "He often visits us, but, do you know,
I've never actually met him. He normally goes straight to
his room and stays there with a case of whisky dumped on
one half of a double bed. He believes, you see, he was
legally married to whisky some years ago. I'll say that for
him, he's the most faithful of husbands. Disappointment,
you know, his whole life's been a sort of expression of a
grudge. You see, he's my husband's twin, but was born just
seven minutes after my husband. That means he missed the
baronetcy by a short tail (it was a dorsal presentation).
But he writes the most charming letters thanking me for a
pleasant week-end. He also sends presents. Those statues
outside are his most recent gift. Strangely enough, the presents are always to my husband, not to me, and I can't
make up my mind whether they're meant to give pleasure
or are intended as white elephants. I suppose he spends
most of his time resenting the fact that my husband got
the baronetcy, then he repents of his hard feelings and tries
to make it up by sending gifts of ambiguous value. He
travels, in his lucid moments, and the presents acquire a sort
of exotic lustre by coming from Easter Island or Corsica. But
they could easily be picked up cheap in the Caledonian
Market. The box-rooms are littered with specious junk.
They gather dust, and my husband soon forgets about them."

"These," said Crowther-Mason, standing at the window, "look a bit too solid for quick oblivion."

"Oh," said Lady Drayton, "those, you see, symbolise the Golden Age, and the Golden Age, as far as my husband's concerned, is any time, so long as it belongs to that perpetually expanding club he calls the past. The present can qualify for membership if it waits long enough. But tell me about Ambrose. Is he fixed up for the night? I'm glad, anyway, he remembered the taboo on spending the night before the wedding in the same house as the bride."

"He didn't remember," said Crowther-Mason, "but I reminded him. He's taken a room at the Crown—that's where he dropped me—but he's coming along, so he says, to dinner."

"That's all right," said Lady Drayton. "It won't be much of a dinner, I'm afraid. The kitchen's holding its fire for tomorrow. Tomorrow brings war on a tough enemy —the entire county and a host of penurious relatives, hungry as quicksand, swallowing bones and all. Now, if you've no objection, I shall leave you. There's a great deal still to be done. You know your room, don't you? I know you won't mind being left alone for a while. A little intelligent silence may be welcome after the week in Parliament."

"I shall stay here," said Crowther-Mason, "and read *The Times.*"

"Do that," said Lady Drayton, "and help yourself to whisky." Nodding, she went out, a trim woman. Crowther-Mason sat in a deep armchair, sighed, then opened the rustling sheets of the top people's paper. He began to read a fourth leader of incredible Elian archness. He sighed again, got up, and helped himself, as Lady Drayton had instructed, to whisky. Soft summer light flashed sharply in the cut-glass decanter. He drank, looking out on Sir Benjamin's statues. They seemed a cheap and ill-sculpted lot.

All the gods were really Vulcan; only Venus—the only goddess there—was at all presentable. Bernard Drayton, Esquire, lying upstairs in his whisky-stupor, could have told an interesting story of their provenance. A slick talker from Catania had talked much of opening a pleasure-garden in Syracuse and had commissioned those statues as heroic garden-furniture. But he had run away hurriedly without either paying for them or collecting them, leaving debts and pregnancies. The stonemason, a man with a squint, had become sick of the archaic smiles of those deities cluttering up his yard. When Bernard Drayton had paid him a visit the stonemason had vilified his own work before this Englishman. "Take the lot," he had said. "Take them out of my sight for ten thousand lire. Bad cess to them. And to him." For the slick talker from Catania had rendered the stonemason's own daughter pregnant, as well as commissioning work for which he had not paid. The stonemason had had a squint, and this squint he had imparted to all his gods—in vengeance or because he believed it to be the ocular norm. The daughter, perhaps in an earlier pregnancy, had been the model for Venus. Crowther-Mason did not know this, but he admired now this goddess smirking like a whore, the archaic smile with its eyes and risor muscles mirthless, endearing in ancient sculpture as the isometrics of Giotto. There she stood, Venus all entire, five fingers reaching out to touch, the other hand protecting the public from the pubic gaze.

"Oh," said a voice, "I beg your pardon. I was looking for Diana." Crowther-Mason turned. He saw a hard-featured woman in her middle thirties, smart in a hard tailored way, impeccably made-up, staring at him. "You," she said, "must be Mr Crowther-Mason."

"None other," he said.

17

"I thought so. You're quite like your newspaper photographs."

"That's rather unkind."

"It wasn't meant to be," she said, coming towards him. "I'm a journalist, and we journalists regard our world as a higher order of reality than what most people call the real." She smiled, a hard smile. "Forgive me," she said. "I doubt if you'll have seen *my* picture unless you read the more saccharine women's magazines. I'm Julia Webb."

"How do you do?" said Crowther-Mason. "As a matter of fact, I have dipped into a few of them. It's important to know what kind of dreams one's female constituents indulge in. And, as a matter of fact, I do remember a face something like yours poised like a queen's or goddess's above some page or other. A page full of answers to anxious enquiries. Would that be it?"

"That would very much be it," said Julia Webb. "I give thoroughly pernicious and immoral advice to young women. I prefer to think of them less as human beings than as pimply parcels of televisual reflexes. Some of them are still innocent enough to believe that even a kiss might infect them with babies. Others are much concerned with the size of their busts."

"Why did you say 'immoral'?" asked Crowther-Mason.

"All restraint is immoral," said Julia Webb. "I follow William Blake in believing that. But my work, God help me, consists in encouraging young girls to be unhappy for the sake of sales and social stability." A vicious vixenish look took over her face. "Sometimes I long to incite elopement, adultery, bigamy. How, sometimes, I should love to see the simpering minxes who flaunt their décolletages on our front covers lose their ivory castles in a salutary blow. 'I've fallen in love with my stepfather,' some of my readers say. I feel like saying, 'Excellent, run off with him.' 'I

18

hate my mother,' say others. 'Put ratsbane in her porridge,' I want to advise. But all the time I must calm them down to uneasy order, accepting things as they are, the ghastly emblem of it all being the coy, arch, vacuous, rouged egg-face on the cover."

Crowther-Mason offered her a cigarette. "We have something in common," he said, lighting it for her. "Chaos should be my constituency. I went into parliament believing in the sanctity of order, but the only order I've ever seen lies either in machines or corpses. The arranging of bones into patterns seems fruitless. Anarchy is more fitting for lives as short as ours. We should look for colour, not form, and learn to prefer toothache to the dead grin of perfect dentures."

"How right you are," said Julia Webb. "Another symbol is, of course, the wedding photograph—bodies encased in frills or tubes, the desperate smile, the wretched couple frozen in a gibber of happiness. You, I believe, are best man tomorrow; I'm chief bridesmaid. Both of us are to officiate at a death, whatever the cards of invitation call it. This marriage is a horrible thing, despite the clang of rejoicing, the rubbing of hands and the festive smell of mothballs. It's gruesome, obscene, a wedding of oil and water, a ball and socket forced into fitting. Forgive me. You're his friend. But, being his friend, you should know even better than I that it will never do. Of course, I'm thinking only of Diana. I know what lies before her and I know what should lie before her. But I can't get out of my head a particular image—the solid-seeming door on the stage-set, seeming to open on to a broad landscape, but leading instead to a whitewashed wall at the back of the stage which says, 'I am reality. All hope abandon. *Ne plus ultra.*' The wall is Ambrose."

"Don't be so morbid," said Crowther-Mason, smiling.

19

"He's all right. His teeth are his own. He's wholesome as fresh bread. Admittedly, he's little enough to offer, except a thorough knowledge of structural engineering. But the time comes surely when a woman prefers a steady job and a life insurance and a bank balance to poetry that won't sell. Romance is all right in its way, but when the new raw lovers have gorged themselves on each other, a paid-off mortgage means more than the passionate clichés that are the mere thin icing on the soggy biological cake. Ambrose will be as good a husband as any. He's no roast pig of richness, crackling with banknotes, but he's comfortably off. He's no Adonis either, but his face will bear looking at. He's neither a fire nor a torrent, but he's not a corpse. You can't have everything. As matches go, it's a good match. The fact is that they've both got a lot to learn, but they can learn together."

"That's just it," said Julia Webb. "Don't you see? Poor little Diana has been learning a bit about life since she went into Fleet Street. She's got talent, that child, and —more important—temperament. The lesson was just beginning; now it's all over. Now she's got to be shut away in a sort of nunnery, without even the spice of celibacy. This Ambrose of yours has been shut away all his life. He's tucked in for a long sleep, and Diana will have to sleep with him. Forgive my frankness, indiscretion, call it what you will. You're his friend and, well, we hardly know each other. But I feel really strongly about all this. I've talked and talked to her, tried to make her think again, but . . . Well, here we are on the eve of the wedding, everything looking as though it's going to go to plan. But she'll regret it, I know she will. She'll remember my words when it's too late." She sucked in a vicious chestful of smoke.

"But, you know," said Crowther-Mason, "there's

something quite charming about a young couple starting off, learning together. I know Diana is, in many ways, older than Ambrose, and Ambrose is old in structural engineering. But in the essentials I'd say they were coeval. I don't suppose they'll know what you and I call reality. They'll know what the newspapers mean by it, the photograph of it. They'll glow in a rose-gold haze. Their nursery will be pink and thoroughly wholesome, thoroughly sanitary. Their ventures into sex will be, perhaps, disappointing, unhandy, fumbling, but crowned by a wholly undeserved aura of charm, as the gateway to clean delicious children. They'll buy little songs and fumble at the keys of the rosewood piano, and laugh a lot, and take in the weekly papers, and gape and then yawn at the television in the corner of a drawing-room hung with Diana's art-school pastiches, till the time comes for the toasting of their household gods in Horlick's or Ovaltine. It's a good enough life. Bless them both."

"God forbid," said Julia Webb. "That's no life for Diana—the long suburban road and the tennis club, the vista of identical aerials, the bookcase empty or containing cookery books, *The Home Handyman* and the life of a popular princess. It's not good enough."

"It's good enough," smiled Crowther-Mason, "and it's rather too late to stop it, anyway. The cake is ready for cutting, the champagne aches to be uncorked. The bride will look lovely. It will be a most successful wedding. Let be."

Julia Webb opened her mouth to say more, but at that moment Diana herself came in, wearing her wedding-dress. It was lacy, silky, pearly, misty, embroidered with fertility motifs of leaf and flower and heads of wheat. Diana herself was a pretty child, blonde, pale and frail-looking. With her was her old nanny, her mouth full of pins.

21

Diana said, "Hallo, Jack. How do you like it, Julia?"

"Enchanting," said Julia Webb. "Really ravishing." Crowther-Mason murmured that it was very pretty. Diana's old nanny, an ageless thin deeply-lined twinkling crone, spat out a pin or two and said, "You mark my words, she'll be the prettiest bride this county will have seen for a long time. Turn round," she ordered Diana. "This bit at the back here. . . ."

"I think," said Crowther-Mason, "you'll be the proudest one there."

"Ah, yes," said the old woman. "And I dearly love a wedding. Weddings, you might say, have been my life, and, of course, funerals. I dearly love both. I like a good laugh and a good cry. That's life, as you might say. Why, I've seen five husbands to the grave already, and, please God, those won't be the last. There's many an old fiddle plays a good tune, as the saying goes. And if Dinah here has as good a life as what I've had, her old nanny—but I'm not so old neither—will be a happy woman."

"*Five* husbands?" said Julia Webb.

"The pleasures of the poor, as you might say, Miss," said the old woman. "Although I read in the Sunday papers that some of these film-stars has had far more, but by irregular means, as you might say. Cheating, I call it. You've got to stick by the rules, or the game's not worth the candle. I never cheated. All my husbands died, and there was always a decent interval, so to speak, before the next. Took, most was, before their time, but, well that's life, as the saying goes, we must go when we're called. And I made them happy. Not even my worst enemy could deny that. Poor Watkins, he was my second, or was it the third? —No matter. We're all as old as each other in the next world, so the Vicar says, and he's a dear man, a fine man, and a lovely preacher. Anyway, poor Watkins died of an

insect in his head. Screaming with agony he was till the
Lord took him. One of the best he was, but—love you—
jealous? He had the flat-iron ready for me every Saturday
when I'd been in the saloon at the Red Lion having my
milk stout—and a fine tonic, that is, puts on flesh, Miss,"
she said to Julia Webb, "and if you don't mind my saying
so, that's what you could do with. Poor Horrabin, my
fourth," she continued, stitching away at Diana's back,
"or was *he* the third?—No matter. Poor Horrabin used to
say, before he fell off his ladder at work—some say he was
pushed, but I'd be the last to deny he drank something
chronic, God bless his dear memory, he always used to say
he liked a bit of something to get hold of. Lizzie Adkins
was always after him, but thin as a rake she was. He used
to say that, if he'd been married to her, it would have
been like going to bed with a bicycle. Anyway, what was I
saying? Oh, yes, poor Watkins would look round from the
public bar with his darts in his hand, glowering like, to
see I wasn't carrying on, as he put it, with Milly Stilgoe's
husband. I never did, of course. Joe Stilgoe was a cobbler,
and he tried to kiss me once with his mouth full of nails.
Jealous Watkins was, but, bless you, I like them jealous,
and a black eye or thick ear hurts less than a cold heart."
She stood up arthritically, her stitching task finished.
"There," she said, "you'll look lovely coming down the
aisle tomorrow. There's going to be some wet hand-
kerchiefs, you mark my words. I always cry when I hear the
Wedding March."

At that very moment she heard the Wedding March,
the Mendelssohn one however, denoting joyful completion.
Crowther-Mason turned to see whistling Ambrose prepar-
ing to stride in by the French windows. "Out," shouted the
old woman. "Out, quick, it's bad luck to see the bride in
her dress before the wedding. You'll be seeing

23

enough of her tomorrow. And," she leered, "after that."

"I'm not looking," said hidden Ambrose. "Is Jack there?"

'I'm here," said Crowther-Mason.

"We'd better discuss tomorrow's arrangements, hadn't we?" said the voice of Ambrose. "What do we do about speeches? Do I toast the bridesmaids, or do you? You know more about speeches than I do," he said plaintively.

"All right," said Crowther-Mason. "I'm coming." And, with a proleptically ministerial bow to the ladies, he went out.

"A dear sweet boy, Mr Ambrose," said the old woman. "Such a nice nature and innocent as the day. Why, to hear him talk, you'd think he knew nothing about it, nothing at all." She cackled. " 'There'll be sweet fruit soon for the picking,' I said to him. And, do you know, true as I'm standing here, he blushed. The boy blushed. And then he said, 'I don't know what you mean.' True as I'm standing here."

"I think," said Diana, "you're wanted in the kitchen."

"Now what makes you think that?" said the old woman, interestedly. "You and me has been upstairs together in your bedroom, and, far as I know, no word passed between anybody in the kitchen and yourself, so to speak. Oh," she said, "I see. I can take a hint as well as the next one. You watch that dress now, Diana, and come up soon. There's still one or two small alterations to make." And, cackling, she left.

2

DIANA took a cigarette from the Chinese puzzle-box by the great vase of roses. "Oh, Julia," she said, flopping into a chair, "I feel so thoroughly washed out, I could sleep for a month. It isn't just tiredness—that's understandable—but a sort of dull palpitation all the time, like a teacher facing her first class, or like waiting to be summoned to an interview. Like standing with your hand upraised to knock at a door, when you know that what's inside is going to be fateful. I keep looking at my watch and thinking, 'This time tomorrow the whole world will have changed.' I can't understand it. I've known Ambrose for a long time, a very long time. Marriage is only a sort of—a sort of regularisation or official recognition, isn't it, of something already accepted. I mean, I don't see why marriage should change my attitude to Ambrose. I can't learn anything new about Ambrose, can I?"

"You're taking a sacrament," said Julia Webb carefully. "This isn't the continuation of a journey you've become used to, timing your body's rhythm to the rhythm of the train, knowing the worn plush you rest on as well as you know your own bed, the read magazines already old and boring friends. It's new: even the station is in a part of the town you've never visited before, though you know the town by heart. The train will steam in with suspicious punctuality. There'll be no trouble with porters or crowds, and the compartment will be empty. As you walk down the corridor you'll notice that all the compartments are empty. You'll feel uneasy. The tables will be laid in the dining-car; the napkins will be spotless; the cutlery will shine like the sun-polished rails. But there will be no service. You'll wonder then what sort of people are driving, fuelling the train, but with no hope of knowing. Then you'll return to your compartment and see *him* there. *Him*, smiling, wearing a new suit, with somebody else's eyes and a mark on his left cheek you'd not noticed before, already a stranger, the years-old deception dropped, his manners charming, the soul of consideration, but not what you ordered. Then you'll realise that there is no destination, that the only place is that compartment, and the only time forever. That is marriage. There's another name for it, but that's Christian and too fashionable to mean much."

Diana writhed on her chair. "You shouldn't say these things," she said. "It's not fair. I'm upset enough as it is. I know you don't mean them. I know you've a flair, a journalist's flair, for words. I know you don't mean to be unkind, especially now on the eve of my wedding. I'm sure I'll be happy. Ambrose will make me happy. A woman's wedding-day is the happiest day of her life. That's true, isn't it? You've told millions of your readers it's true. I shall be happy," she said unhappily. "Say I'll be happy," she pleaded.

"Words are funny things," mused Julia Webb. "To a writer they're perhaps the only reality. The meaning doesn't count. You repeat a word to convince yourself it *has* meaning. You repeat it again and again till the meaning loses its meaning. The word is reduced to a series of glottal events. Are you sure now you know what you mean by 'happy'?"

"You're so clever," sighed Diana, "that you can make what seems thoroughly solid to me melt to a weak trickle. You can drain my skull of what seemed part of the bone. But I know, or think I know, what I mean by being happy. Being happy is being with him. I want to be with him. I'm glad I'm marrying Ambrose," she said defiantly.

"You protest too much," said Julia Webb. "Let me show you what could be in store for you. You're young, you're very pretty and, I think, very talented. Your work's been widely praised. You'll make a name. You've hardly started yet. You'll meet people, charming people, people infinitely urbane and erudite, important people, people compared to whom Ambrose will sink to the level of a gauche nail-biting schoolboy. You'll travel. Journalism is itself a big world, but also it's the opening to a bigger, realler, world. You can develop your personality, a personality that, otherwise, will be aborted, will lie in the drawer like an unfinished letter, smell on the dish like a stained half-eaten apple. This is the chance to be complex, infinitely sought-after, infinitely desirable. Those are the fruits that will come after your flowering. They wait patiently, now."

Diana got up and walked over to the French window. Venus smirked at her. "This," said Diana, "is rather horrible of you. The temptation is bad enough, but to leave the temptation till now, as my hand's on the door. . . . The first act's set and the audience settles with programmes and chats through the music. This is quite diabolic."

"Let me show you," said Julia Webb, "what's in store for you. Though," she said, "in a way, you know already. You know that it's death, but death, you know too, can be made quite pleasant, and pain can become not merely tolerable but desirable, given time. The price you'll pay for being what you call *happy* is the sinking of all that's you, a life-long death. Imagine you're learning another, more primitive, language, and perpetually, with a bad accent and a weak vocabulary, you're translating for his benefit. The meanings are bound to change—they become simpler, coarser, not what you intended, and some things can't be translated. All the real things, the things you want to say, are starving inside you, screaming to be fed with expression. And you know, the gardener cut off from the garden, that the flowers are dying, and there's not a thing you can do. That's going to be your life. Then death comes: then you'll convince yourself that all you thought important isn't really important—that time is really the tradesman's calendar hanging, spotted with fat-stains, above the electric cooker; that space is what you can traverse in your thirty-to-the-gallon car. And it all ends in the headlight-flooded garage door. Eleven o'clock. The key in the lock, the pink cretonne in the bedroom. 'Bedtime, darling.' 'Terribly sleepy, darling?' 'Do go to sleep, darling.' 'No, darling.' 'Please darling. . . .' "

"Stop, stop," said Diana, almost crying with nerves. "I never knew you could be as cruel as that. You make me feel as though I'm committing a sin, a sort of adultery. My body feels unclean. I seem to be suddenly alone." She shivered. Outside the sun still played and the birds twittered, the statues smiled.

Julia Webb came closer. "Listen, Diana," she said. "There's no need to feel alone. I can help you, Diana. You'll wonder why I left what I had to say till now. It's not really cruelty, please believe that. But if I'd fed you for months, since we first became friends, with this—well, what some would call poison, you'd have had time to generate an antibody, to inoculate yourself. Now is the big moment, when the stage is set, when you're dressed like a sacrificial, very virginal, lamb, to reverse the soldier's oath, to make this rejection of the sacrament itself somehow sacramental. Leave by the front door, not the back. The bands will be playing, banner headlines blaring the news, the floods full on you. You'll never doubt then that you were right. You'll see it as something historic, dramatic, significant, final, irreversible. Do you see what I mean?''

"And then what?" said Diana. "After the decision, there remains tomorrow. When one's finished deciding, one has to act. There's got to be a time and place to act in."

"Leave," said Julia Webb, "time and place and everything to me. We can be happy together, if that word has meaning. We can go away together—it's easy. I've money; I'm not dependent on anyone for a living. We can go abroad—to France, if you like; I've a villa in the South— for as long as you like, or at least till the tongues stop wagging. We can do a lot together, and you'll have a chance to work, unhindered by babies and shopping and a man breathing down your neck. You can allow your art to develop. I can look after you, you need looking after. I'll be more than a husband or a friend. . . ."

"I know now," said Diana, "that you've always been a stranger. I've never really known you. I don't understand you. Your words somehow make sense, but not a sense I've ever known before. I feel a kind of elation, but whether good or bad I can't decide. I can't think. What are you doing to me?"

"Nothing," smiled Julia Webb. "I'm only, so to speak, a voice speaking for you, speaking your own desires. I'm giving location to those desires. I'm fixing the image on the canvas. The hands of the clock parade, long to be chosen for action. Choose now. Act." They both started at the sound of loud singing. "Damn," said Julia Webb. "It's your father coming. You'd better go up to your room." Diana hesitated. "Go on," urged Julia Webb, "I'll follow you up."

Sir Benjamin's bushy rock-face was vinously flushed. "Ah, young woman," he said. "I've just been in the kitchen." He belched slightly. "Most satisfactory. An admirable pastiche of the past. Let bells and bellies rejoice tomorrow. Pardon. And, whether it's the right time of day or not, I've sampled the champagne. I've had a bottle. Wine, young woman," he swayed, "makes blood, and blood makes history, and blood is conspicuously, pardon, conspicuously absent today. Anaemic, that's what we are." He began to sing:

> "Heroes are dead to them,
>   They worship TV stars.
> Deep thinking, deep drinking
>   Give way to coffee-bars."

He performed a small ungainly dance. "You see them," he said, "goggling at the box that's made for goggling. There the drained, the vampire-sucked simulacra, pardon, simulacra, the stewed-out fibres of the new bloodless mythology ogle and amble and posture and moo. And there they are, chewing cheap chocolates."

"Yes," said Julia Webb. "Now, if you'll excuse me. . . ."

"Wait," said Sir Benjamin, holding up a traffic-policeman's hand. "You see them in the pictures, too, with dovetailed sticky paws. And they let that dirty conjuring trick, persistence of vision, weave them a flat-nosed, odourless heaven, ultimate reality, of which this coloured, stinking, various, delightful, painful world is but a copy. Pardon. God help us," he rumbled, seeking help from a side-table. "God help us. The country's sinking in a sea of giggles of girls in late-night buses. We're suffocating in a mound of cardboard pies with a spoonful of wormy-minced guts inside them. Blood. Pardon. When people lose blood, they

30

see visions. I shudder to think what visions coil up from the fumes of the tea in the in-trays of these dentured myopic executives who are already working on the first draft of the millennium. Pardon. With its hearty pipe stuck into rotting teeth, table tennis for all and fishpaste sandwiches, and scoutmaster yarns about clean living. To hell with clean living," he shouted. "Corpses are washed, and while the earth is dirty let our feet be dirty too."

"Please," said Julia Webb, "if you'd excuse me. . . ."

But Sir Benjamin had already turned to confront Ambrose and his best man, coming in by the French windows, chattering. Julia Webb dashed out and climbed at once to Diana's bedroom.

"It's absolutely incredible," said Crowther-Mason. "If I hadn't seen it with my own eyes I'd say that it could not possibly have happened."

"Pardon," said Sir Benjamin. "What exactly are you talking about? Where's that young woman gone to?"

"We couldn't have imagined it," said Ambrose. He was a ruddy light-voiced young man. "I mean, we were both there. I saw the finger move." He pushed his hand forward, supinated. "Like that." He made his second finger roll back to the palm. "With the ring on it. Incredible"

"Now," said Sir Benjamin, "what exactly is this?"

"Oh, there you are, sir," said Ambrose. "The most incredible thing happened. Out there in the garden."

"It was like this," said Crowther-Mason, "if I may tell the story."

"We were in the garden, you see, sir," said Ambrose, "admiring your statues."

"You haven't been touching those statues?" Sir Benjamin rumbled threateningly. "Speak carefully, sir. My veins brew blood still."

"We haven't exactly been touching them," said

Crowther-Mason. "But we were walking round the garden, you see, sir, discussing tomorrow and all the various arrangements. Then Ambrose asked me. . . ."

"I asked him about the ring," said Ambrose. "I wasn't quite sure what finger to put it on. No man is ever sure, sir. But women always know, from the age of two onwards they know. But I didn't know." Sir Benjamin, frowning, made thoughtful glove-finger-smoothing movements. He nodded.

"Never mind about that," said Crowther-Mason. "Now, sir, as it happened, we were standing in front of one of your statues."

"The statue of Venus," said Ambrose.

"The statue of Venus," agreed Crowther-Mason. "And, as you know, sir, one of her hands is held straight out, like this." He demonstrated.

"Straight out like this," agreed Ambrose, demonstrating also. "Each finger separate from the others. So I did the obvious thing."

"He slipped the ring on," said Crowther-Mason.

"I slipped the ring on her finger," said Ambrose.

Sir Benjamin boiled and hiccoughed. "Can't you, pardon, leave well alone? Haven't I enough to cope with, keeping that foul-mouthed dish-slopping cretinous hank of tatters that calls itself a maid away from them? Are they, pardon, doomed to desecration? An engineer and a progressive politician—I might have known you'd join the illustrious company of those who treat the past as a sort of gutter to spit into. All right. We know where we stand. It's a challenge. Pardon. I accept the challenge. I have a shotgun. Pardon. From now on those statues are going to be guarded."

"But that's not all," said Ambrose.

"*So I did the obvious thing.*"

33

"No," said Crowther-Mason, "I'm afraid that's not all. And here's the incredible part."

"I couldn't have believed it," said Ambrose, "if I hadn't seen it."

"What, sir?" said Sir Benjamin beefily. "What couldn't you have believed? Pardon."

"The finger," said Crowther-Mason, "slowly crooked itself, like this, back to the palm."

"Like this," said Ambrose, "very slowly."

"But deliberately," said Crowther-Mason, "like an obscene invitation. A finger made of stone, mark you, with the wedding ring on it. The finger-tip touched the palm."

"It curved back slowly to the palm," said Ambrose, "and then stopped."

"It couldn't, of course," said Crowther-Mason, "move any further."

"With the ring on it," said Ambrose.

"And," said Crowther-Mason, "we can't get it off."

"Ah." Sir Benjamin sat down. "Aha. Pardon. This may excite your wonder, the incredulity of your anaemic age which explains the miraculous away with algebra and washes the blood out of everything. But to me it isn't surprising. No, not surprising at all. I've read about such things. In the past these things were always happening. There used to be, you know, men with three heads and trees that could preach sermons. And, once upon a time, you could actually fall off the edge of the earth. But now we have the safe railed-off present. These things don't happen any more."

"But," said Crowther-Mason patiently, "this *has* happened."

"Those effigies," said Sir Benjamin, "epitomise the past. Pardon. That large godlike humour. Hurricane jokes. All your textbooks torn to confetti and sent spinning down the singing gutter. Where are your laws now, eh? Your bridges," he said to Ambrose, "may all collapse tomorrow. The House of Commons," he said to Crowther-Mason, "may spin like a drunkard's bedroom. The past has come back, pardon, in a tiny tendril of humour. Ah. Aha."

"Listen to reason, sir," said Ambrose. "Please. That ring cost money. But, of course, that's not really important. What is important is that the wedding's tomorrow afternoon. We want the ring. Without the ring there can be no wedding. May we break the finger?"

"Old age," said Sir Benjamin, breathing deeply and slowly, "is a time when deafness brings its blessings. I didn't hear what you said then. You have another chance."

"May we break the finger?" asked Ambrose again. "We could do it with a hammer."

"I thought, sir," said Sir Benjamin, "that those were the words. The world is all before you. By God, my hiccoughs have gone, and no wonder. As for 'break', 'break' is a trull of a word, it will take in everything. Waves, dawns, news, wind, hearts, banks, maidenheads. But never dream of tucking into the same predicate my statues as object and that loose-favoured verb. That would be a most reprehensible solecism." He leapt up and roared, "Leave those damned statues alone, if you want it in plainer language. Don't meddle with the past," he suddenly whispered. "It's alive," he said in crescendo, "aching to electrocute. It's a fire with a trick of burning. Or, rather, shall I say I am those things? I, I, I." He bellowed the pronoun like an affirmation. "Ah," he said, more genially. "Aha. Hahaha." He went out, hahaha-ing.

3

AMBROSE RUTTERKIN was a decent young man with an honest structural engineer's face in which bewilderment now patently showed. He said: "Now what the hell are we going to do? The old boy means it, and I'm not prepared to argue out the metaphysics of it with him. Can we get another ring, in time, I mean? The wedding's at three. I suppose we *could* drive into town and back again. But you know, frankly, I don't see why I should have to fork out for another ring, when there's a perfectly good one sitting out there on that piece of rotten statuary. I'm not made of money, you know."

"Perhaps," suggested Crowther-Mason, "we could get a secondhand one from some local shop or other."

"There's a small shop in the village," said Ambrose, "a sort of general store. It sells dusty cough-drops and thick twist and toilet-rolls and yellowing postcard views of Hovis signs and—oh, other down-to-earth essentials. But rings—I hardly think they think that sort of commodity likely to be asked for very often. It's a respectable village."

"Well, how about Pigstanton?" suggested Crowther-Mason. "That looks like a biggish sort of town. There must be a jeweller there."

"There is, in a way," admitted Ambrose. "But you've got to catch them between two fires, as it were. They've just had their latest. Luckily they were insured."

"If the worst comes to the worst," said Crowther-Mason, "we must drive to London, that's all. But Diana might get a bit annoyed if she finds out you married a statue, even if you didn't mean it. It would be best if we could get one fairly quickly, without too much fuss. Perhaps we could borrow one."

Lady Drayton came in, saying, "All this seems very strange. Ben's just been telling me what happened. But, if I were you, I shouldn't attempt to get that ring off. I know my husband."

"Could you, Lady Drayton," said Crowther-Mason, "possibly lend us a wedding-ring?"

"I'm awfully sorry," she said. "I keep many things in reserve—candles and bottled plums—but as for rings, no. My own would have to be charmed away, like a wart. I and it are quite inseparable."

"If it's rings you're fussing about," said Sir Benjamin, coming in fussily, "stop fussing. There are plenty of rings on curtains, and taps have washers still."

"Diana's nanny," suggested Crowther-Mason, with hope. "She must have *lots* of rings."

From the door Julia Webb looked in sardonically. "Oh, Miss Webb," said Lady Drayton, "something rather awkward has happened. The wedding-ring has been, shall we say, lost. Do you happen to have one? Oh," said Lady Drayton. "Oh, what a very unfortunate thing to say."

"Because, after all," went on Crowther-Mason, "her husbands must have come to her complete in every detail."

"This," said Julia Webb, as she sauntered in, "is a matter of purely theoretical interest. You won't need a ring.

There's not going to be any wedding. Diana has changed her mind. She asked me to tell you."

They stared at her.

"You know," said Ambrose, "just for a moment I thought you said that there's not going to be any wedding."

"That's just what I did say," said Julia Webb. "The wedding is off. Diana has changed her mind."

"Really, Miss Webb," said Lady Drayton, "this heavy-handed sort of jape is in rather bad taste, especially when we're all wondering what to do about a ring."

"This is not a joke," said Julia Webb. "It's true. Diana has changed her mind."

"But this is absurd," said Lady Drayton. "Where is Diana?"

"Diana," said Julia Webb, "is asleep. She had a splitting headache, and no wonder. That girl's been going through tremendous nervous strain. I made her take three of my sleeping tablets. You won't wake her up, not before nightfall."

"I," said Lady Drayton, "will have a word with that young woman. She won't get away with this."

"Her door's locked," said Julia Webb. "She's fast asleep. If you speak your monologue through the keyhole, she just won't hear you."

"We'll see," said Lady Drayton. "We'll see." And she tore out.

"You won't do any good," said Julia Webb.

"Hell and damnation," stormed Sir Benjamin. "She's changed her mind, has she? The little slut, the impious young bitch. Trying to break her father's heart, that's what it is. Think of that damned food cramming the larders. Can that change its mind? That food must be eaten, those bottles must go back empty. And if nobody else feels like a celebration, I'll force myself into the mood, I'll think of something. I'll commit bigamy, I'll marry my wife again (there's no law against that) and if she won't have me I'll get my brother to marry. I'll wake him up just enough. He won't know what's happening. I'll find somebody in the village for him. Damn and blast it. Anger makes me hungry. As far as I'm concerned, the wedding breakfast has already started. I'm late for the first course." And he rumbled out.

"Well, Ambrose," said Crowther-Mason, "I don't quite know what to say. You know her better than I do. Do you think she means it?"

Ambrose looked dazed. "I don't know her at all," he said. "I see that now. If this is part of the pattern that's Diana, I don't think I know anything. I suppose I ought to go up to her room and bang and bang till she'll wake up and listen to sense. But what is sense? I'm learning something. I'm learning that the current was carrying me, and not my own oars. I've learnt that I can't row. And, now I come to think of it, there doesn't seem to be a file in my brain that contains a letter about marriage. Did I ask her to marry me? I can't remember. Marriage was just something understood. I don't think either of us ever questioned it before. I've known Diana a long time. At least, that's what I thought till just now. God, I feel terribly confused. Is it flaw in the metal? Flaw in the blueprint? Back to the draughtsman's board. I must tease out the knots, if I can find fingers. I'm going back to the pub. I think I'd better be alone."

Crowther-Mason watched him shamble out. He turned on Julia Webb, but she got in first. "Well," she said, "do you remember? 'Anarchy is more fitting for lives as short as ours.' Your words, I think. Here's a nice helping of chaos for you. Now, if you'll excuse me, I must telephone."

"You're an evil woman."

She walked, nonchalant, over to the instrument. It had a doll-cover, something Diana had made as a child.

"I see," said Crowther-Mason. "A nice helping of chaos that you've cooked. Now you can impose form, fill up the void in your own way. Now we've got to sit back and watch your own crooked little cosmos emerge. You break a limb in order to reset it in such a way as to perpetuate lameness. Clever. A good way to spend a holiday."

"Hallo," she said to the telephone. "London. Revelation six double six." She turned back to Crowther-Mason. "Yes, a holiday. That's what I'm going to arrange now."

"You're an evil woman" said Crowther-Mason. "You must find this prospect rather refreshing. Refreshing after the humdrum task of keeping in repair a house you'd hate to live in. After expending your cosmetician's skill on a raddled face whose every wrinkle is your idea of beauty."

"Miss Cawthorne, please," she said to the instrument. "Oh, is that you, Stella? Julia here. I'm going to take that holiday. . . ."

Crowther-Mason stalked out through the French windows, after Ambrose. He heard Ambrose's car singing forlornly off to his loneliness.

4

WHEN Lady Drayton failed to communicate with her daughter she became remarkably and, to Julia Webb, somewhat frighteningly, calm. She was even polite to Julia Webb, which was even more frightening. At dinner Crowther-Mason talked about art and Sir Benjamin, eating, talked about nothing. In the drawing-room after dinner, when the two women were together, it had to be left to Julia Webb to re-open the matter of Diana's sudden decision. Lady Drayton said:

"I apologise for the dinner. Tomorrow I hope you'll see what we really can do. This was a sort of Lenten mortification preceding the feast-day."

"Your sack-cloth is beautifully tailored," murmured Julia Webb.

"I believe," said Lady Drayton, "it was John Keats who coated his tongue with pepper before he drank claret. He could savour the coolness better. In the same way, you know, I believe in long engagements. They sharpen the lovers' appetites like a winter walk. Then they can really relish the fire in the bedroom. Will you have more coffee, Miss Webb?"

"Thank you. You seem confident, Lady Drayton, that the

wedding is still going to take place. Diana was definite, perfectly definite, I thought. She's not the sort of person who's likely to reverse a decision, is she? You know, better than I, how headstrong she is."

"Well," said Lady Drayton, "as far as reversing decisions is concerned, she's reversed her decision to marry."

"Oh, that was never really a decision, was it? It was always understood, or so I've been told, that she should marry Ambrose. Isn't that so? Didn't they both grow up with the idea, a sort of toy that outlasted infancy. A sort," she said, "of limbless teddy-bear. It's something neither of them ever questioned. She, I suppose, took it for granted like the picture above her bed. But now she's seen that picture in new surroundings. She's switched on the light now. Now she can smile at the nursery dream."

Julia Webb did not smile.

"You mean, of course," said Lady Drayton, "that you switched on the light for her."

"So you *have* spoken to her?"

"No, I haven't," said Lady Drayton. "But I'm not altogether blind, you know. You're a woman of the world, Miss Webb. For good or ill, you're a person of considerable strength and magnetism. A girl like Diana was bound to sit at your feet. You've been kind to her, you've helped her —without condescension. No wonder she adores you. When she's been home at weekends we've heard your name from her lips so often that I've been not a little jealous. A sort of blast of trumpets and a gigantic shadow—those have heralded your approach. Well, you're here at last. Here to take Diana away, if you can. You beckon, and Diana follows. You say, 'Do this', and she does it. You're a woman of the world. How do you expect a mother to feel in these circumstances?"

"I've only done what I thought to be a duty." Julia Webb lighted a cigarette, one taken from her own case. She

43

did not offer the case to her hostess. "Diana mustn't enter this cotton-wool world of drying napkins and fireside slippers. Blue eyes," she sneered, "and blue heavens, kittens with blue ribbons. You, as a mother, ought to know her gifts. Would you have her sacrifice what might well be a brilliant career?"

Lady Drayton smiled. "Our four eyes are open," she said. "We both know how to assess Diana's talent. It's a little talent, you know that as well as I. It won't take her very far. She draws very prettily: can we say more than that? It's the sort of talent that a girl fifty years ago would have taken in her stride, along with needlework, singing and child-bearing. No, you surely can't be so ingenuous as to suppose that I suppose your motives to be, well, altruistic."

"I meant what I said," said Julia Webb. "It's wrong, it's positively sacrilegious, to yoke Diana to a dull thing like Ambrose. She'll shrivel, she'll decay. I can suggest other plans for her."

"For both of you, you mean," said Lady Drayton. "You'll go away, the two of you, you making all arrangements— reserving berths and booking hotel rooms, firing Diana with yet more adoration at your command of foreign languages, your way with porters, your mastery of the menu and the wine-list. Then Diana will become aware, oh, ever so slowly, of your true intentions."

"I don't," said Julia Webb slowly, "quite follow what you mean."

"Corruption," said Lady Drayton, straight out. "A slow silken technique of infinite patience. A fine-drawn filigree cage, sumptuously appointed, but still a cage. The door, of course, wide open, but with no possible exit."

"I," said Julia Webb, flushing, "am not that kind of person. I offer friendship, that's all. You're looking for far too much."

"There's no danger of eyestrain," said Lady Drayton, "when one comes face to face, as I do now, with a naked hungry will like yours."

"Stick to the simple issue," said Julia Webb stoutly. "All this is irrelevant. You're over-dramatising. Reconcile yourself to the fact that tomorrow will see no wedding. Diana won't change her mind. Diana will be gone. The only thing you can do is to cancel your arrangements."

"Oh, yes," said Lady Drayton, "that's just what you want, of course. A headline, like a black rainbow, over the county, and a startled henroost of fluttering flurrying aunts and cousins. Oh, no, Miss Webb. The story's by no means over. Let the organ play, let the church be filled. We'll cross the bridge when we come to it."

"The bridge," said Julia Webb, "is already down. Diana and I will be gone in the morning."

"The night's long, you know, even in summer."

"I have to admire you," said Julia Webb. "The fighter I understand. I've had to fight often in my time against odds that seemed hopeless. But this refusal either to plead or to wrestle—that's a little frightening."

"Why should I fight against you?" said Lady Drayton. "What right have I? Diana must find things out for herself, in her own way. Besides, you may think this a foolish belief, but I have the conviction that there are forces on my side, which I think to be the good side, and that those forces are twitching into life this very evening. Don't ask me to explain what I mean, because I can't. You must just wait, that's all, just wait."

Spatchcock, in clean evening apron, came to the door to say that the Vicar had come. "Show him in, please," said Lady Drayton.

"That's someone you can tell," said Julia Webb. The Vicar came in, hearty, all smiles, arms out in greeting.

45

"I shall tell him nothing," said Lady Drayton, "till there's something to tell. Good evening, Vicar," she said. "This is a pleasant surprise."

"Not really a surprise, is it, dear lady?" said the Vicar. "The hymns. The hymns. Nothing has been done about choosing the hymns. I'm afraid I forgot and you forgot and everybody forgot. Still, you must forgive this late intrusion. You must be too busy to think about hymns. I have, of course, my own suggestions. I promise you I shan't keep you more than a minute or two."

"The Vicar," said Lady Drayton. "The Reverend Chauncell. Do you know Miss Webb, Vicar? She is, among other things, Diana's chief bridesmaid."

"How do you do?" cooed the Vicar.

"Would you care for some coffee?" offered Lady Drayton.

"Thank you," said the Vicar. "That would, in fact, be most welcome. This is very seasonable weather. The procession of the seasons seems to skirt England now, as though England were only a sidestreet and unworthy of processions. Every month we always expect to be winter now, and we're seldom disappointed." Lady Drayton gave him coffee and he sipped it loudly. "I hear rumours, by the way, Lady Drayton, rumours that must be completely without foundation, because otherwise I know you would have informed me at once, rumours that Diana is ill and confined to her room. Rumours travel fast in a village, Miss Webb. I take it, Lady Drayton, that the rumour is completely without foundation."

"The rumour's quite false, Vicar," said Lady Drayton. "Diana is indeed confined to her room, but she's confined herself. Far from being ill, she merely refuses to go on with the wedding."

"Oh, is that all?" said the Vicar with relief. "Oh, well, that's nothing to worry about. I'm so glad it wasn't

46

something serious. This last-minute recalcitrance is very common, very common indeed, Miss Webb. It means she's taking the whole thing soberly. I well remember the night before I was ordained. I entertained, for the first time too, very considerable doubts. The whole solid structure of revealed religion just lay in ruins about me. The Bishop laughed when I told him. He said it was a good sign, thoroughly healthy. So I just stopped worrying. Now, Lady Drayton, shall I just give you my suggestions as to the hymns?" He put down his coffee-cup and took out a fistful of papers from his left-hand pocket.

"I just can't understand you people," said Julia Webb. "Diana's said, as definitely as it's possible to say anything, that she's not going to marry. Yet you people go on," she went on rudely, "as though she hadn't uttered a word. What sort of deafness is this? It's true, I tell you. Diana's not going to marry."

"There now, Miss Webb," soothed the Vicar, "there's nothing to worry about. Weddings make all of us a little nervous. I blush like a girl when I read the marriage service still, after all these years. It's vicarious excitement. You wait now. You'll be there in church tomorrow, as pretty as a picture. You shan't be disappointed."

"I won't be disappointed," agreed Julia Webb. "Excuse me." And she went out, thunder in her face.

"Poor girl," said the Vicar. "One could almost think it was *her* wedding."

"She's one of the heretics," said Lady Drayton. "She's one of that sect that doesn't believe in marriage. I wonder if she inherited that from somewhere."

Sir Benjamin and Crowther-Mason walked in, smelling richly of port and walnuts. "That girl looked green, Winifred," Sir Benjamin said, "quite green. I thought those mushrooms weren't too fresh. Oh, hallo, Vicar. Nice of you to call. Have some brandy. You know Crowther-Mason, don't you? This is the Reverend Chauncell." And he started to pour brandy.

"I know Mr Crowther-Mason by repute, of course," said the Vicar. "I think I saw you on the television set of one of my parishioners. I was invited to dinner, but much of the dinner consisted of looking and listening to you on the television. You spoke very good sense, I thought."

"Still, it was wrong of me to get in the way of your dinner," said Crowther-Mason. "Now, if this is the Rev. N. A. Chauncell, I'm happy to be able to express my appreciation of a little monograph I read with great enjoyment. *Sin and the Good Life* was the title, I believe. I was greatly struck by it. A rather unusual subject, if I may say so, for an Anglican clergyman."

"Oh," said the Vicar, "sin is my hobby. Not, of course, the commission of sin, ha ha, but the study of it. A vicar needs distractions from work which becomes increasingly secular. I think about sin with a kind of wistful nostalgia, like a long-dead summer of ginger-beer and bluebottles. Nobody sins any more, and sin, after all, ought to be my business. I envy doctors; they have diseases. But what have I except the same old round of joyless fornications, mechanical slanders, malice clothed as self-righteousness? I see some point in people doing wrong so long as they do it zestfully. But where there's no zest there's no sin. Really, we might as well be back in the Garden of Eden. And, indeed, when I look at the photographs in some of the Sunday papers I often think we are."

"It's true enough," said Crowther-Mason. "The concept of sin seems to be dead. It's been expelled from the Garden. Freud and Marx hold up their flaming swords. But surely it's a good thing?"

"It's an atrocious thing," said the Vicar. "It's killed

both kinds of good living. It's removed a dimension from our lives. We've all lost that incense-laden thrill we used to get from the exciting knowledge that, if you pulled up the floorboards, you would find a deliciously bottomless pit. What have we instead? Right and wrong, with their inter-changeable wardrobes, and the police-courts, temples of a yawning, neutral god with a relish for disinfectants." With a pleasant smile he raised his brandy to his lips, as with a relish for it, as in a silent toast to sin. But he spluttered with shock, and all gasped with surprise, as the French-windows were shiveringly pushed open and Ambrose entered, nearly dead on his feet, paper-faced, trembling with terror, saying:

"Give me a drink, for God's sake."

"Ambrose," said Crowther-Mason, taking him over to a chair, "what on earth—"

"Have my brandy," said the Vicar, christianly. "It's purely marginal with me, I can assure you." And he thrust the balloon glass into the shaking hands of Ambrose.

"Thank you," said Ambrose, polite in his terror.

"Now then," said Sir Benjamin bluffly, "what's hap-pened? Come on, spit it out." An unfortunate expression, for Ambrose at once sprayed the area of the room immedi-ately in front of him.

"Let me get my breath," he gasped.

"Troubles," said Lady Drayton, "seem as gregarious as buses. What *has* happened, Ambrose?"

"Give the boy a chance," bullied Sir Benjamin. "Come on now," he bullied, "*what happened?*"

"I don't know quite how to start," said tremulous Am-brose. "It's so incredible, you see. And, now I come to think of it, it's rather embarrassing. To talk about, I mean. Could we, I mean, could I just tell Jack here about it?"

49

"I see, I see," saw Sir Benjamin. "Winifred, my dear, we could do with more coffee."

"I'll ring for some," said Lady Drayton.

"No, damn it," said Sir Benjamin. "Go and make it yourself. You make such good coffee."

"Ben, you jolly well know I don't."

"Not normally, no," said Sir Benjamin. "But on this occasion, yes. Go on, my dear, I'll tell you all about this in bed."

"Oh," said Lady Drayton, "very well. You know my extension number." And, making herself very tall, she walked out.

"Now," said Sir Benjamin, eagerly, "it's all men together."

"Tell us what happened, Ambrose," said Crowther-Mason with politician's patience.

"Well, you know," said Ambrose, his tremor subsiding somewhat, "it's still pretty embarrassing."

"Oh," said Sir Benjamin, "I see what you mean. Don't worry about the Vicar, my boy. He's High Church."

"My dear boy," said the Vicar, "no priest is capable of being shocked, not after studying the lives of the patriarchs. Now tell us all about it."

"All right," said Ambrose. "Well, as you know, I drove straight off to the pub as soon as I'd heard what Diana felt about me, or about the wedding. I had a couple of double whiskies and a sandwich and then went up to my room. You can imagine how I felt."

"Yes, yes," said Sir Benjamin. "Never mind about that."

"I felt," continued Ambrose, "that, as the guests had been invited and Daimlers had been laid on, and all that food, it seemed rather a pity to disappoint everybody. They could at least have a funeral."

"Cut out the self-lacerations," said Crowther-Mason. "Just tell us what happened."

"I went to bed," said Ambrose. "My head was splitting, but I wanted to think things over. I drew the curtains to shut out the idiotic light. I undressed and lay down. Then it happened."

"Yes?"

"Yes?"

"Yes?"

"I know you won't believe me," said Ambrose. "I can't believe it myself."

"I can believe anything about that pub," said Sir Benjamin. "Go on."

"I was wide awake," said Ambrose. "The room was pretty dark. I lay on my side."

"And then?" said Crowther-Mason.

"There was a woman lying beside me."

All relaxed. "A woman?" said the Vicar.

"Yes," said Ambrose. "Even in the dark I could tell it was a woman."

"Well," said Sir Benjamin, "that's nothing to worry about. Either you were in the wrong bedroom, or the landlord's becoming more enterprising."

"What happened then?" said Crowther-Mason.

"She spoke."

"Of course she spoke," said Sir Benjamin. "Women always speak."

"What did she say?" asked Crowther-Mason.

"It was all so quick," puzzled Ambrose. "She spoke in a foreign language."

"What language was it?" asked the Vicar.

"Well, as you know," said Ambrose apologetically, "I was on the Science Side. I was never much good at languages. But it didn't sound like any language I'd heard

51

I undressed and lay down. Then it happened

before. Not any language you hear on the Continent. If anything, it sounded like Greek, but not the sort of Greek people learn at school. It sounded as though she meant it."

"And then what?" asked Sir Benjamin.

"I was too petrified to move. Then she came closer. Now I could definitely tell it was a woman. She spoke again, but this time in English. A queer sort of English, rather hard to understand."

"But what did she say?" asked Crowther-Mason.

"She said something like this: 'You can't marry that woman. This is a monogamous country. You're married to me.' It was queer that she got that 'monogamous' into it, because it sounded as though she didn't know much English."

" 'Monogamous'," said the Vicar, "is Greek."

"So she was Greek, was she?" said Sir Benjamin. "Well, well. I suppose the new vice laws are driving some of them out of Soho. Driving them down here," he said, as though a whole new world were opening up. "Well."

"What did you do then?" asked Crowther-Mason.

"I leapt up out of bed," said Ambrose, "and switched the light on. Then I looked. . . ."

"What happened? Who was she?" asked the Vicar

"There was nobody there," said Ambrose. "The bed was empty. There wasn't even the mark of any body except my own. She wasn't there any more. She'd left no trace. She'd gone, just like that." He clicked his fingers.

"I see," said Sir Benjamin. "So it was *she* who was in the wrong room."

"No, no, no," said Ambrose. "She couldn't have got out. The light switch was by the door. The window was only open a little way at the top. In any case, I should have seen, shouldn't I?"

"Did you," asked Crowther-Mason, "look under the bed?"

"There was nothing, or rather nobody, under the bed."

"This," said the Vicar cheerfully, "sounds like nerves, my dear boy, just pre-nuptial nerves, exacerbated by over-indulgence in spirits."

"I thought you'd say that," said Ambrose. "I wasn't tight. My nerves were steady as a rock. I tell you, there was definitely a woman in that bed. But," he ended lamely, "she just went out like a light when the light went on."

"Lights?" frowned the Vicar. "Spirits?"

"What did you do then?" asked Crowther-Mason. "Did you complain to the landlord?"

"No, no. I threw these clothes on, as you see." All now saw clearly that Ambrose had put a suit on over his pyjamas, that his laces were not tied, that he wore no socks. "Then I got the car out of the garage and rushed straight here."

"Crooked, probably," mused Crowther-Mason, "not straight. A most extraordinary thing. . . ."

"Tell me," said the Vicar, "did you notice anything at all, well, *strange* about the atmosphere?"

"How do you mean?"

"Well, was there, for example, a sort of aura, a strange glow in the room, or an unusual smell, perhaps?"

"Unusual smell," pondered Ambrose, "unusual smell. Well, yes, now you come to mention it, there *was* an unusual smell. How can I describe it? It was a tang like the taste of oysters, if you know what I mean."

"Perhaps," said Sir Benjamin, "she'd been eating oysters."

"That's hardly likely," almost snapped Crowther-Mason. "There's no R in the month."

"Now I come to think of it," said Ambrose, "I got a sort of illusion that the room was overlooking the sea. The sort of feeling of a first night on a Brighton holiday. I half-expected sand in my toes and buckets and spades on the stairs and seaweed in the hall and drying rompers. Just like that. As though I were in a seaside hotel. Yes, that was it. The smell and feel of the sea. The room was full of it. It was rather exhilarating at first. And then, of course, I was so scared that I stopped noticing it."

"The smell of the sea," said the Vicar, with tones of fear swelling up. "God help us."

"Is it something bad, then, Vicar?" asked Sir Benjamin.

"I apologise for that involuntary ejaculation," said the Vicar. "It meant nothing. What I had in mind hardly seems possible. Perhaps I'm expecting too much." He shook himself sensible. "This took place in an inn by a major road. Radio music and light flashed by in cars urged on by their drivers to quite unurgent appointments. Everything seems solid. This is the age of the television cowboy serial and supermarket. But I thought for a moment of demoniac possession."

"What do you mean by that?" almost screamed Ambrose. "Am I going mad or something?"

"Not mad, no, not mad," soothed the Vicar. "But perhaps possessed by devils, like the Gadarene swine."

"Oh, come, Vicar, really," rumbled Sir Benjamin. "Surely that's going a bit too far. This poor lad's upset enough as it is."

"Think for a moment," said the Vicar. Instinctively he got up and placed himself behind a tapestry screen, a frail pulpit. "Take off," he adjured them, "your weekday suits of incredulity. These things *do* happen. In the spiritualistic séance the voice of little departed Effie or big departed Aunt Edith is often the voice of the devil. Yes, the devil. The devil undoubtedly exists. He normally shows himself as a sort of quick-change artist, a comic with a rich patter but a loaded slapstick, or else something damnably desirable.

But look for the trademark. He always gives himself away in something. Like this, perhaps. But why the smell of the sea? That, brethren, I cannot understand." He came to, apologetic. "I'm sorry," he said, "to use that term 'brethren'. I just wasn't thinking."

Ambrose was open-mouthed. "You mean," he said, "it wasn't a woman at all?"

"Precisely," said the Vicar. "A demon, if you like."

"But why?" Ambrose was almost crying. "What have I done? The whole day's been a long succession of shocks. First the ring, then Diana. Now you talk about devils." He shook over to the decanter and poured himself more brandy.

"This is only supposition, of course," said the Vicar. "But can you blame me for half-hoping I'm right? You want an explanation. Very well, here's an explanation for you, one in full regalia, but affording us at the same time a glimpse of the posterior of ultimate reality. That's one way of putting it." He coughed. "But here I am, with my forty years as a vintner, dispensing watery tea on the vicarage lawn. Down in the keyless cellar the bottles mature ravishingly. There's work for me at last. But I can't, for the life of me, think why this should have happened. What big sin? What provocation? Dear, dear. This poor boy. . . ." And he put his hand on Ambrose's head as if he had been translated into a confirming bishop.

"Look," said Crowther-Mason. "Wait. You know, this is all quite incredible, but I think I begin to see a sort of connection. It's crazy, I know, but somehow it seems to make sense."

"Out with it, out with it," boomed Sir Benjamin.

"There's a picture by Botticelli," said Crowther-Mason. "As a matter of fact, I was talking about it during dinner, but nobody seemed to be listening. It depicts the birth

"the laughing-eyed delight of gods and men, waiting for Ambrose."

of Venus. She's rising out of the waves. You can smell the sea, almost, just by looking at that picture. What is the legend now? Something about sea-foam breaking out of the mutilated member of Tellus, and Venus being born out of that foam."

"That," said the Vicar, "is indeed what the Greeks believed."

"Well," said Crowther-Mason, "you remember the other queer thing that happened today?"

"Oh, God," said Ambrose.

"What queer thing?" asked the Vicar.

"Ambrose and I," said Crowther-Mason, "were in the garden. You've seen Sir Benjamin's statues, of course, Vicar. Well, Ambrose, rehearsing for tomorrow, put the wedding-ring on the appropriate finger of the statue of Venus. Now this that happened next was quite incredible. The finger closed to the palm with the ring on it. We couldn't get it off."

"Venus?" breathed the Vicar.

"Yes," said Crowther-Mason, "and now I don't know whether to laugh or cry. Ambrose is really married. It was the goddess herself who spoke. She told no lie."

"No," said wide-eyed Ambrose, backing away from Crowther-Mason. "No. No. No."

"Oh, yes," said Crowther-Mason. "You've been trapped into marriage. That finger looked very inviting, too inviting. Your bride is a pagan goddess. In the little bedroom over the public bar, over the darts and dominoes and detergent, over the luke-warm bitter and the packets of crisps, Venus was waiting for the dark. Foam-born Aphrodite," almost shouted Crowther-Mason in a kind of manic joy, "the laughing-eyed, delight of gods and men, waiting for Ambrose, waiting to claim her marital dues in Ambrose's

58

single bed (fifteen shillings the night, including breakfast).
Oh, Ambrose, Ambrose, what can I say?"

Whatever he could say, nobody else could say anything.
The clock ticked. In the distance a late cuckoo clarinetted
Delius or Beethoven. Night had arrived.

5

AMBROSE broke. His back to the wall, as though hunted, he said: "You've said enough, damn you. You were always the same. Those dormitory japes at school were never particularly funny. Slugs in the bed. Booby-traps. Andrews Liver Salt in the chamber-pot. Those were bad enough, blast you. Now you've gone a bit too far, damn your eyes. God knows I can take a joke with the best of them, but at a time like this, when I'm feeling like death.... Is everyone turning against me? I thought," he said, sadly, reproachfully, "you were my friend."

"Ambrose," said Crowther-Mason, "listen a moment...."

"I suppose," said Ambrose, "I'm the laughing-stock of the village now. That local whore you bribed into my bed for a couple of bob or a gin and bitter lemon or whatever it was—she's not likely to keep her trap shut."

"You've got it wrong," said Crowther-Mason, "all wrong, Ambrose. It was a sort of joke, I suppose, a cosmic joke you could call it, but believe me, Ambrose, please believe me, I had nothing to do with it. Nor had any of us here."

"You seem," said Ambrose, "to know enough about it."

"That was just a bit of deduction," said Crowther-

Mason. "Sit down now. Have some more brandy, Ambrose. You're overwrought, that's your trouble."

Ambrose began to shake his head madly. "Too late," he cried. "Too late. I'm sick of the whole damned lot of you. Humiliation, that's what it is. I'm going to wipe my hands clean of the whole boiling of you. The wedding's off. There's nothing for me to stay for."

"Listen to reason, Ambrose. . . ."

"To hell with reason. To hell with you. To hell with Diana. To hell with me. Literally."

"Now, Ambrose, don't start thinking of doing something foolish."

"I'll do what I want to do." He began to leave. Dignity was diffcult. He had a fair amount of brandy in his stomach. His shoe-laces were not tied. He nearly tripped. A shoe came off. Dancing on one leg he tried to put it on again. "Damn you, blast you," he said thickly, dancing. Crowther-Mason tried to grasp him and bring him back. "Take your filthy hands off," he said. He tore himself off and out through the open French-windows. It was a warm plummy night.

"Out of the way, Sir Benjamin," said Crowther-Mason urgently. "I want to follow him." Sir Benjamin said:

"Leave him alone. Let him cool off a bit. He won't do any harm to himself. Not the type."

"Please. . . ."

"No." Sir Benjamin barred the way to the French-windows. "I want you to tell us all about it. A damn good joke, though a bit ill-timed, I should have thought." Crowther-Mason made for the door. "I wonder who the girl was?" mused Sir Benjamin. "A game one, no doubt about that. Lizzie Hawkins, perhaps. Or Nancy Pluckett. Anything for a lark, nearly anything. Sorry, Vicar. Forgot you were there."

"I've been thinking it over," said the Vicar. "It seems plausible enough. More than plausible, thoroughly cogent. I used to study this sort of thing, you know. The origin of devils. The ancient gods never died. They joined the opposition when the new administration took over. Devils were once gods. Devil—the very term means 'little god'. This poor boy's bewitched. Possessed by a little god. Or goddess. But they can't have sex, can they? But, of course, it's the form they take. A devil disguised as a goddess. Dear, dear, dear."

"We'll get a different story out of him," said Sir Benjamin, "when he cools off a bit. He'll be back in no time at all, you mark my words."

Ambrose was. He burst in again, more terrified than before. "She's there," he cried. "She's outside. She followed me. Don't let her in. Don't let her get me. It's the same one. She spoke to me. The same words. Let me hide. Help."

Crowther-Mason came in through the drawing-room doorway. "Good," he said. "I thought you'd think better of it. Now sit down and try and be calm about the whole thing."

"She's out there, I tell you," cried Ambrose, pointing wildly. "Out there in the dark."

"I think," said the Vicar, "one of us ought to go and see."

"You'd better go, Crowther-Mason," said Sir Benjamin. "I'm pouring out more brandy for everybody."

"You'd have more influence, Vicar," said Crowther-Mason.

The Vicar sighed. "Very well, if you say so." He walked out stoutly. He walked in stoutly. "There's nobody there," he said. "Nobody at all."

"Perhaps," said Sir Benjamin, "it was somebody sleep-walking. Perhaps they've gone back to bed."

"You're a bit overwrought, Ambrose," said Crowther-Mason. "Sit down. Look, here's some more nice brandy for you." Ambrose flopped down in an armchair. He took the brandy. He drank it as if it were water.

Sir Benjamin, his own brandy in his hand, sniffed vigorously. "Ah," he said. "Can you smell what I smell?"

The Vicar sniffed. "Fish?" he said.

"Like," sniffed Crowther-Mason, "a whelk-stall at Brighton."

"Ozone," sniffed Sir Benjamin.

"The sea," sniffed the Vicar.

Ambrose screamed. "I can smell it, too." He tried to get up from his chair, but Crowther-Mason pushed him down. "She's in this room. Don't," he yelled, "let her get at me."

The Vicar took Sir Benjamin's glass of brandy and handed it to Ambrose. "Drink this," he said. "Try and keep calm. A spirit will never appear in the light. Remember that. As long as the light's on there's absolutely no danger. The spirit world is frightened of the light. Have you got that? Do you understand that? Good." Ambrose nodded, shook his head, nodded. He drank his brandy thirstily. "That's a good boy," said the Vicar. "Everything's going to be all right. Now, gentlemen," he said, "we must season our admiration for a while. . . ."

"There's certainly enough salt in the air," sniffed Sir Benjamin.

"We must start work," said the Vicar. "At once. We must exorcise this spirit. Let me see, let me see."

"Exercise," said Sir Benjamin. "I see what you mean. Cold baths and plenty of exercise. That's what my scout-master recommended, I remember. A way of putting down excess sexuality, that's what he used to call it. Going to be a bit difficult, though, to exercise a thing like this." He sniffed. "This sea air's as good as a tonic," he said. "If

The Vicar sniffed. "Fish?" he said.

this goes on we can cancel our trip to Clacton. Brandy," he said, turning the decanter upside down. "Somebody seems to have been drinking a lot of brandy. I'll have to get more." He went out singing.

"What we have to do," said the Vicar, "is to perform a ceremony. We must drive out the devil with appropriate incantations and so forth. But I shall have to get certain things from the Vicarage. It would be quicker, obviously, if somebody could drive me there. This poor young man? Dear, dear, obviously not. Perhaps you, Mr Crowther-Mason?"

"Don't leave me here alone," said Ambrose, though with rather less terror than before.

"I've told you," soothed the Vicar. "You're completely safe so long as the light is on. Now, there's absolutely no time to lose. We must start praying at once, of course. We can pray on our way to the Vicarage. You pray, too," he said to Ambrose.

"You don't mind if we take your car?" said Crowther-Mason to Ambrose. "Is the ignition-key in it?"

"Don't be long," said Ambrose. "For God's sake."

"Light," said the Vicar patiently. "You have plenty of light."

"Supposing the lights fuse?" said Ambrose.

"The worst is the most that can happen," said Crowther-Mason impatiently. "Relax."

6

SIR BENJAMIN did not come back. Presumably he had gone to wake up Lady Drayton and tell her the strange story, perhaps even to advise that she come down and smell the ozone as something that would make her sleep. She would, naturally, resent being awakened to be told that. Perhaps he had lost his way in his cellar. Perhaps he had gone for supper to the kitchen. Anyway, it seemed a long time to Ambrose that he was alone. The smell of the sea was still there, as strong and bracing as ever. Courage, however, was now flowing into the arteries, the brave spirit doing its work. He sought more brandy, remembered that that was what Sir Benjamin had said he was going to get, so contented himself with a half-tumbler of Cointreau. There were a few books in the drawing-room, including a volume of Shakespeare's poems. He took down this volume and began to read *Venus and Adonis,* remembering that he had not been allowed to read it at school. He began to understand why. Sensuality, eh? Sensuality. Adonis, it struck him, was a bit of a fool. Pursued by the goddess of love and beauty, preferring to hunt wild boar. A bit of a bore himself, or a boor.

But, of course—it began slowly to dawn on Ambrose—

was he himself not precisely in the position of Adonis? He was not hunting, however. He had not preferred to do one thing rather than another. He had merely run away. As he thought muzzily about this, Diana tiptoed into the room. Queen and huntress, chaste and fair. Fair, yes. Chaste, presumably yes. Queen? Nonsense. Huntress? Tonight there was only one huntress. Ambrose pretended to be asleep. As soon as his eyes closed he felt a presence take advantage of that private twin darkness: he seemed to feel a kind of total embrace of his entire body, exciting and frightening. He opened his eyes to a roomful of light and Dian. standing by him.

"Hallo, Ambrose," she said, somewhat shyly. She was dressed in her going-away clothes.

"Oh, hallo," he·said without getting up.

"You won't think too badly of me, will you, Ambrose?" she said. "I haven't much time to talk. Julia's waiting with the car. We're flying over to Paris tomorrow morning. We're spending the night at the airport hotel."

"How about your people?"

"I think they're both in bed. At least, I heard voices from mother's room. I'll write to them. I couldn't bear to say much to them now. Besides, it would be hard to make them understand in a few words, and I've only time for a few words. I needn't say much to you, need I? We've known each other such a long time. I think you know what I'm doing and why I'm doing it."

"Hm," said Ambrose. "Your brilliant career, you mean?"

"Don't be bitter, Ambrose." She sat on the arm of the armchair opposite his. "This isn't a matter of being selfish, if that's what you think. Julia says it would be far more selfish to give it up, selfish to more people."

"Some women," said Ambrose, "have found it possible to combine marriage and a career. Some have ridden the

67

two horses most gracefully." He felt that he could tonight, for some reason—the spirit in the bedroom, the spirit in the decanter—find something like eloquence.

"No." Diana shook her head. "Something has to give. Julia says that my art must come first. It's only fair, she says, because so many women have no creative talent at all. Unless, of course, you can call the ability to produce children a creative talent."

"The aesthetic pot," said Ambrose, "calling the biological kettle black."

"You mustn't be bitter, Ambrose. Why, you yourself have said—often, too—that I have, well, *you* called it genius. Yes, genius. Do you remember the time when I had my first exhibition? Oh, I know it wasn't London, only Pigstanton. I know it wasn't much of an exhibition really. I was only nineteen."

"Two years ago."

"That's a long time in an artist's career. I've learnt a great deal since then. But you remember that the local critic was quite warm in his praise. He said I'd go far. But you thought that wasn't enough. You said that people ought to recognise true genius when they see it. You wrote to the *Advertiser*."

"I nearly did," said Ambrose. "I very nearly did. Have some Cointreau?"

"No, thank you. And I don't think you'd better have any, either. You look quite flushed."

"That, if I may say so, is my affair. Listen, Diana. I too am two years older. Two years have taught me that lovers make poor critics. Hyperbole is a lover's coin, even for small purchases. Ever since Adam woke to press his lips, as on morning tea, on his costal emanation. . . ."

"Ambrose," said Diana sharply. "It strikes me that you've been drinking. Really drinking."

"Diana," said Ambrose softly, "I *am* drinking. Really drinking. Let me continue. Or, rather, let the brandy and the whisky and this sweet stuff borrow my larynx for just a little longer. Ever since, as I say, that doubtful experiment in Eden, all women, by some miracle of penetration or extension of the textbook laws, have been the most wonderful. All your attributes, all your little achievements, have been, to me, superlative. Superlative or unique."

"You've never spoken like this before," said Diana in some wonder.

"I've never had so much alcohol before. To continue," Ambrose was up, glass in hand, walking the room as briskly as his untied shoes would let him, "we lovers, God forgive us, inflate all language. Supposing some other woman had painted those pictures. Pictures." He snorted. "Those slick, polished, sedulous acts of homage to Cézanne and Picasso. What would I have said then, eh? I'd have said that they were very pretty. I'd have left it at that, always the little gentleman. Please don't mistake me. I meant what I said at the time. But love, you know, is really a fever. One's temperature rises, one's head is suffused with hot air. One's words are turned to balloons. And then, of course, it becomes too late to prick them: they fly out of reach." He looked up at the ceiling, really seeing balloons. "There they are," he said, "floating up there, mocking me. And there's no possible airgun."

"Now," said Diana, arms folded grimly, "you're seeing things."

"Oh," said Ambrose, "I'm seeing a lot of things, but, for the first time in your presence, not through the poster-paints of delirium, but in the morning light of crapula." Crapula, yes, he thought; but tomorrow morning was still far, far off.

"So," said Diana, anger beginning to poster-paint her

fresh young cheeks, "the fever's cooled, has it, my little convalescent? It's as well this has happened. Julia, as always, is right. Marrying you would have been digging my own grave."

"Does it matter what I say?" said Ambrose, his arms out like a 1929 mammy-singer's. "I'm much too weary to protest love again, now, at this late hour. But I *would* say that a two-eyed love is possible, that the other sort is no better for being myopic, that a pair of spectacles, a diopter or two of correction, isn't in any way incompatible with two people living together and being happy."

"It's too late," said Diana, "for the oculist."

"And another thing," said Ambrose, "while the strong right arm of these various spirits supports me—let me say this: I've put up with a lot. I've been the pursuer, willing to tolerate spurious art-talk and coffee and cooing over canvases, your unwashed artistic friends, unshaven or bearded, though they always looked unshaven, even the women, and your new set, reeking of self and halitosis, brown-fingered dyspeptic Fleet Street touts with typewriters in place of the higher cerebral centres. And, of course, Julia."

"You leave Julia out of this," she said dangerously.

"I'd be glad to," said Ambrose. "I've pursued you through those stucco labyrinths just to be near you. I could cut out the other presences like interfering signals on a radio, to tune into you. But I'm a little tired of being the perpetual pursuer."

"You the pursuer!" scoffed Diana. "God, don't make me laugh. This is a new note. Namby-pamby Ambrose seeing himself as a cartoon hero, a sort of hairy faun, a satyr in the passionate forest, muscled and marrowy and masterful, chasing nymphs. Don't make me laugh. You've tagged around, with spaniel eyes, saying nothing. The art school crowd used to wonder what ever I saw in you. You were

70

always a bore. It was always humiliating to have to say who you were when you went out of the room for a moment. I had to say, 'My fiancé.' You were usually introduced, but always forgotten. People would be quiet for a second when I said that, and then talk about something else. You the pursuer! You should thank me for charity. A flavourless engagement, exciting as boarding-house cabbage. I've put up with that out of charity. I've rejected other offers out of loyalty to the schoolroom or out of habit. Or pity. What other woman would look at you?"

"You mean that rhetorically," said Ambrose, pronouncing the word carefully. "Rhetorically. But, believe it or not, it has a positive answer. A woman *is* after me. *I'm* being pursued."

"If," said Diana, "you mean that insipid half-wit, Cynthia Boydell, I suppose she just about qualifies. That's no particular distinction. She's getting to an age when she'd chase anyone. That's just what she seems to be doing."

"No, not Cynthia." Ambrose shook his head and found it difficult to stop. He must be careful. It was the Cointreau that was going to cause the trouble. "Not Cynthia. Though she at least has no pretensions to painting."

"That," said Diana, "is evident from her make-up."

"I mean someone else," said Ambrose. "Someone beside whom all women are flavourless." Careful, careful. "Beside whom they become as ineffectual as the moon. The moon," he said poetically, "when it's seen as a nail-clipping of light on a scorching day." Hurray.

"Who is this paragon?" asked Diana. "Some goose, I suppose, has broken your arm with a swan's wing." She sniffed. "Funny," she said. "Very fishy. What's been going on here?"

Should he? Yes, he would. "A goddess," said Ambrose. "That's what she is, a goddess."

"The alcohol will be writing sonnets for you soon." She sniffed again. "Queer. Come on, let's have the other clichés now."

"She *is* a goddess," said Ambrose, drunkenly and stoutly. "How else can you describe a goddess except as a goddess? And she wants me. Yes, she wants me. She's the pursuer. She doesn't think I'm a bore. She's the epitome of woman, not," he said, "not a second-hand bundle of coy erogeneity draped," he said, "in an all too diaphanous robe," he said, "of pudeur."

"Don't try those weapons with me, Ambrose," said Diana. "You can't get me back that way."

"My poor child," said Ambrose loftily, "don't flatter yourself. This is a key which may really lock the door. Don't look back after you've gone and ooze a horrible sap of pity over my memory. Don't defile me. I've reached full stature at last, and without your help."

"Are you telling me the truth?" said Diana, blazing. "Is it true what you said? Have you been with another woman?"

"I have been in bed," said Ambrose, "with a goddess."

"Where? When?"

"Oh, this evening. At the hotel. Not more than an hour ago. A goddess, remember that, a goddess." Ambrose smirked.

"Right," said Diana. "Right. I can only thank God I've found you out in time. I knew you were *low*, but I didn't think even you capable of that. In bed with another woman. On the eve of our wedding. Right."

"But it isn't the eve of our wedding."

"It was," said Diana. "You scum. You unutterable swine. You sexless pig."

72

"Sexless? Sexless? Really...."

"Sexless? *Sexless?* Really. . . ."

"The lowest of the low, that's what you are. I've a good mind to tell my mother."

"Oh, do that, please. And then say you're going off with a notorious lesbian."

"I loathe you."

"I'd no idea you felt so strongly about me," smirked Ambrose.

"Go to hell. Go to hell." Diana looked charming, all fire.

"*You're* going to hell, my love," said Ambrose. "You may not know it, but you are. Leave that to Julia. To Julia. Haha." He began to recite, with wide gestures:

> "Whenas in mink my Julia goes,
> Then, then, methinks, how fast it flows,
> That liquefaction of her nose.

Ha ha. Ha ha ha ha ha."

"This is definitely the end," said Diana. "I thought we could part friends, but this is definitely . . ."

"I've heard plenty about Julia," said Ambrose. "Plenty and plenty. I may be moronic, but I know what she's after. There is, for instance, a little pub in Soho. It's called . . ."

Diana came up to him, tight-lipped, and gave him a fair open-handed smack on the cheek. His world glowed for a moment red, red in little pulsing circles. "You," she said, deliberately, "are thoroughly loathsome, hateful, and I mean hateful. I never thought I could feel this way about anyone. You're a cesspool, you're a sore, you're a gutter. I'm well rid. This is really the end."

"And you," said Ambrose, "are a perfectly wholesome but rather insipid creature. An undressed salad, that's what you are. A good plain English dinner. You're neither ugly nor beautiful, you're wholesomely neutral. You're two-dimensioned and monochrome. You bore me rather. I'm well rid. Now I'm taking to solid food. The illness is over."

She stood undecided, almost ready to cry, in a woman's rage that could so easily topple over to snivelling and wanting to be taken into somebody's arms. But she steeled herself, trying to be a goddess, chaste, fair, dignified. Still, tears wanted to flow. She sniffed, but this time not at the puzzling sea air, and ran on her pathetic high heels out of the room, calling, "Julia! Julia!"

"Haha," said Ambrose triumphantly. "Hahaha." Then, tottering, and not sure whether he could see straight enough to read, he went back to *Venus and Adonis*.

7

WHERE were they? Where was Jack? Where was the Vicar? Ambrose felt uneasy, but it was the uneasiness of one whose stomach is brooding over a doubtful burden. The house, too, seemed so terribly silent. He had finished *Venus and Adonis* and was now puzzling through *The Phoenix and the Turtle.* Shakespeare's birds twittered and barked through his head. One bird spoke to him, an old woman of a bird, sharp-nosed and bright-eyed. It was Diana's old nanny, standing over him, solicitous. "I heard you was on your own, Mr Ambrose," she said. "Look what I've brought for you." It was a cup and saucer, something viscid, brown, steaming. "A nice hot cup of cocoa. Hot and strong, there's nothing like it last thing at night, especially when you're feeling a bit low and restless like. I've just had mine. Here, now, drink it while it's hot."

Ambrose gulped, his stomach swam at the prospect. Could the stomach then hear? Did it have ears? How many? "Very kind of you, nanny," he said. "But, honestly, I don't think I could." He wondered whether he ought to dash out on to the lawn. But no, the dark. It was all very well to preen oneself about being hunted by a goddess, here in the cosy light, but perhaps the Vicar knew what he was talking about. Perhaps it was not, after all, really a goddess. He felt very drunk and queasy.

"You ought to get something on your stomach," said Diana's old nanny. "Grief's a bad supper, Mr Ambrose. Are you sure now I can't get you something from the kitchen—a nice ham sandwich, perhaps, or perhaps I might cook you a kipper?" She sniffed. "Not that this place doesn't smell of kippers. Sir Benjamin, I suppose. Or perhaps it's just my imagination." She sniffed again. "Bloaters more than kippers, I'd say."

"I can't smell anything," said Ambrose. He just did not dare. The smell of a ship's galley, fish being prepared, Biscay bumping and howling outside. No, no.

"I shouldn't worry too much," said Diana's nanny comfortably. "Dinah was always a bit headstrong. Full of passing fancies, as you might say. When she was little she was always changing her mind. You couldn't keep pace with her, little madam as she was. A good smacked bottom was the only way to get her to make up her mind. It's what she could do with now."

"She's made up her mind," said Ambrose. "It can't be called back." Perhaps if he had another glass of Cointreau. . . . No, no. But there was some whisky over there. He tottered over to the decanter.

"She'll come without calling," said the old woman, "sooner or later, if I know anything about her. If she didn't want her sago pudding as a child I never used to force her. She'd eat it sooner or later. Like a dog coming back to its vomit, if you catch my meaning."

"I catch," swayed Ambrose, "your meaning." No, no whisky. Advocaat? A nice custardy soothing beverage. Custard. He contemplated custard a moment. No, he

77

didn't feel sick. Curious. He poured himself Advocaat. It coiled sluggishly into his tumbler.

"And," said the old crone, "supposing she doesn't? There's plenty more fish in the sea. The sea," she sniffed. "That's what it is, the sea. Imagination's a funny thing. Must be because of talking about holidays in the kitchen over supper. A fine young man like you, Mr Ambrose, shouldn't have far to look for a wife. And it doesn't really matter who you marry, not really. It's the marrying itself that counts. You know, Mr Ambrose, when I look back at my husbands I sometimes can't remember which was which. I only noticed the other day while I was looking at an old photograph album, I only noticed that it was Watkins that had the moustache and not Horrabin. And Horrabin had a wooden leg. I'd clean forgotten." She cackled like an old oboe. "But there, what does it matter? We're all Adam's children, and Eve's too. Male and female created He them, says the Vicar. That's a lovely saying, and I've never stopped being glad of it."

Good glowing stuff, this Advocaat. Still, he felt depressed. He looked at the old woman and decided he would take her into his confidence. "Easy," he said. "Surprising how easy it all is." He stopped in front of a picture, one of Diana's—an improbable still-life in which half a guitar was being fried with onions and dead-sea fruit. "Damn silly picture," he said. "Yes, nanny," he continued, swaying towards her. "Marriage is very easy. You don't have to do a thing about it. Like catching mumps. A ring and something to put it on, that's all you need. But, take warning from me, take warning. Next time you marry, don't marry a statue. Causes too much trouble for everybody. Never dream of marrying a statue."

"Bless you," she said, smiling, "they're all statues until you warm them up. Horrabin was. Had no natural affection at all, so to speak. More feeling, there was, in his wooden leg than in him. For all the good he was at the start I might just as well have married one of them heathen statues of Sir Benjamin's out there." She cackled. "And his feet was always like ice."

"That's just it," said Ambrose excitedly. "That's just what happened today. I've married a statue."

"Beg pardon, Mr Ambrose?"

"I've married a statue."

She patted his arm maternally, saying, "You've been worrying too much, that's your trouble, Mr Ambrose. Here, drink up this nice cup of cocoa before it gets cold. You'll feel better then."

"Listen," said Ambrose urgently. "You must listen. You must believe me. I put a wedding ring on the finger of that statue of Venus there in the garden. Yes, I did. Ask anyone. And you know what I found in my bed?" He felt very drunk. He would not be able to last much longer.

"Now sit down," she insisted. "In this chair." Ambrose was only too ready to sit. "And drink this nice . . ."

"There they are," he said wildly, waving towards the garden. "Four for a penny. Any one you like. The whole damned lot of them. Roll up, roll up. Jupiter and Mercury and Mars and Pan and Apollo. Any one you fancy. Just shove a ring on and he's yours."

"Just you have a little sleep," said the old nanny, with kindly anxiety. "You're not used to all the drinking you've been doing. That's what causes the trouble, Mr Ambrose. Drinking on an empty stomach, that's a terrible thing."

"Do you," said Ambrose, almost supine in his chair,

79

—*the gleaming white shapes in the odorous dark.*

"do you believe? Believe in the—" it was a difficult word to get out—"the shupernashural?"

"Beg pardon, Mr Ambrose?"

"Shupernashural?"

"Oh, I see what you mean. Well, I believe in the cards and the tea-leaves and Napoleon's Book of Fate, of course, like anybody else," said the old woman. "And Old Moore's Almanac, of course. But I wouldn't say as how I was really what you might call superstitious."

"Shupershtishous," said Ambrose. "What I shay izh true. Perfectly true. Ashk Shir Benjamin. Ashk Jack. Ashk the Vicar. It'sh true, I tell you. My wife izh heathen goddesh. Thouzhandzh and thouzhands of yearzh old. Venush. Goddesh of Love. Married." He passed out completely, snoring.

"Poor lamb," said the old woman. "There, there, sleep it off. You'll be all right when you wake up." She patted him. Then she went to have a look, standing by the open French-windows, at the white-gleaming shapes in the odorous dark. It was a lovely night, a night to stir up love in anyone's veins, however old and varicose. In the old woman's memory stirred gobbets, not merely of residuary amorousness, but of old tales told at school. There was one tale, she seemed to recollect, of a god coming down to earth in the guise of a swan or a bull. She didn't fancy a bull much. And some story also about this same god dressing up as a shower of gold. It was most certainly a lovely night. The earth, she might have thought, lay all Danae to the stars. It was the head god, the boss. She chuckled, looking at the snoring Ambrose. "His missis could give me a few years," she said to herself. Jupiter, that's who it was. A more friendly relationship existed, like, in the old days. A bull, a swan, a cloud of gold. He didn't seem to have known

81

the virtue of moderation. She must go out and have a look at those statues, she thought, and see whether Mr Ambrose had been speaking the truth about this business of the ring. She herself eased an old gold ring, Horrabin's, off her gnarled finger, as she walked out into the fragrant amorous dark.

8

AMBROSE lay flat out, dead to the wide. The twin private darks of his closed eyes invited the goddess or whatever it was to come and take possession, but there was a great sea of electric light islanding him, insulating him. The tendrils of embrace were too weak to disturb him in his sleep, but he had odd amorous dreams, of a voluptuousness not previously known to him. He was chasing nymphs through sun-shot woods, and not one of the nymphs was Diana. He was both amazed and delighted at the hairiness of his thighs. He played a lazy tune that sinuated from C sharp down to G natural and back again. Astonishing that he could flute so lazy a cantilena while chasing nymphs. But the chasing was an airy chasing, requiring no effort. The nymphs giggled and turned into trees, into water, into reeds by the water's edge. Harp-music of water rippled over his flute-tune. "I desire," he seemed to be saying, "to perpetuate these nymphs. So clearly bright is their legerous incarnation that it voltiges in the air, air that is somnolent with tufted sleep. Did I love a dream? My doubt, a heap of ancient night, achieves itself in many a subtle ramification which, while remaining the true woods themselves, proves, alas, that I offered myself quite alone the false ideal of roses for triumph. Let us think about things. . . ."

He wandered, chasing lazily, fluting. Then there came the vision, the terrible vision, on the slopes of Etna. Love's lava. The queen! He panted to embrace, the flute getting in the way. And then it suddenly wasn't a dream. He knew he was really opening his eyes and that it was real darkness that surrounded him. He was smothered in a presence, odorous, damnably desirable, blindingly bright and yet black. He couldn't get out of it. He didn't want to yield, because yielding would mean the end of him, Ambrose Rutterkin, the moderately successful structural engineer, with a good firm, a fine future. He knew that it might be good that that should happen, but the habit of being himself was too strong. "Help!" he cried, transfixed, sober, awake. Nobody responded. Diana's nurse was in the garden, far out of earshot, choosing a god. Sir Benjamin was bumping about the corridors, roaring, seeking with blind hands for the fuse-box. Lady Drayton pulled the bedclothes over her head. Diana and Julia Webb were miles away, travelling in a swift Renault Dauphine towards London, Julia Webb occasionally taking a hand off the wheel to pat the knee of Diana.

The Vicar and Crowther-Mason were in difficulties. As Crowther-Mason drove skilfully and with speed from the Vicarage to the hideous Gothic mansion where Ambrose shouted impotently and with decreasing volume, both he and the Vicar became aware of interference. Birds were fluttering against the windscreen. Birds fluttered in their eyes, blinding them. Yet what seemed to be a whole aviary resolved itself, ever and again, into a mere pair, brace, couplet.

"They're pigeons!" cried Crowther-Mason.

"No, no, not real birds at all," gasped the Vicar. "Devils in the guise of birds. Pray, pray hard." He clutched his case of exorcisation tools to his breast, praying. One of the devil-birds, as in retaliation, then dropped a large earthy mess into Crowther-Mason's face. Blinded completely, he steered wild. All about his head were moaning and whirring attackers.

"Watch out!" cried the Vicar. "God help us!" Crowther-Mason tried to reassert control of the car just as they headed straight for a dry ditch. Wiping dove-mess out of his eyes he saw what the headlights showed him. He braked too late. Quite softly they landed at an angle of nearly seventy degrees, the pigeons cooing and dancing triumph in an ordered flutter above them.

They got out with difficulty, the Vicar not being as young as he used to be. "Come on!" urged Crowther-Mason. "Things are really starting now!"

"I can't run," groaned the Vicar. "I just can't." They walked as fast as the Vicar could, still with the doves moaning and whirring about their eyes and ears.

"Hurry," said Crowther-Mason, taking the Vicar's arm. "Look, the place is in darkness. All the lights have gone." They hurried towards the black heavy pile, all that was left (except for a measly few thousand invested) of the first baronet's original fortune. The wrought-iron gates (infangthief and outfangthief in heavy balls on the gate-posts) were open for their hard-breathing entry. The villainous gods glowed faint in the dark. A bull seemed to bellow in the air above them. "Impossible," gasped Crowther-Mason. The doves fluttered off in panic. One star seemed to glow brighter than a star should glow, it seemed to give off heat. "Quick, now, quick." They reached the French-windows. They

"Impossible," gasped Crowther-Mason.

entered. The smell of the sea, smell of all the herring-shoals that ever were, hit them harder than before, and this time they seemed to hear the laughter of waves breaking. "Light," groaned the expiring Vicar. Crowther-Mason struck a match. The Vicar opened his case and took out candles. With one candle alight, the smell of the sea seemed to recede somewhat. They desperately lighted candle after candle and disposed them about the room, recklessly dripping wax on to the polished surfaces to make, in the absence of sconces, the candles stand.

"Thank God you're here," whispered Ambrose. "I don't think I could have stood much more."

The Vicar got his breath back slowly. "We might have known," he said, "that something like this would happen. A good thing we brought these candles. My parishioners are always complaining about what they term my Romish innovations. By that they chiefly mean candles. But I believe in candles."

As from afar, the voice of Ambrose came from his gaping mouth. "I believe in candles the lighter almighty creator of light upon earth."

"Poor boy," said the Vicar. "Involuntary blasphemy. Anyway, now we have light, and where there's light there can be no evil. How do you feel, my boy?"

"Limp."

"That's to be expected," said Crowther-Mason. "Have some brandy, if there is some brandy."

"I don't want any brandy," came the feeble voice. "Deck me with a sprig of holly and set me alight. Never again. Never, never again."

"We couldn't help this delay," said the Vicar, taking out a holy water sprinkler. "Diabolical interference all the way back from the Vicarage," he explained. "And I'm afraid your car is lying in a ditch. We're here anyway. It's not easy to read in this light, and my eyes could be younger. Now where is that book?" He rummaged among the things he had taken out of his case —sprigs of garlic, a palm crucifix, a bottle of Jordan water. He picked up a thick black volume and, peering with old man's eyes, leafed through it.

"Do you need any help?" asked Crowther-Mason.

"It's enough that you're here as a witness," said the Vicar. "I'm going to recite the words of exorcism. They're Latin, I'm afraid, and that wouldn't greatly please my parishioners. But the devil's conservative: he clings to the old faith. Now let me see, let me see. We should notice almost immediately the dissipation of this diabolical odour. . . ."

"You know," said Crowther-Mason, "I always thought a fishy smell was something you could use to drive out the devil. Because a fish is a Christ-symbol. Isn't that so?"

"You see?" cried the Vicar. "The forces of evil are trying to take possession of you now. Trying to persuade you that there's no evil here. Come, now. Empty your hearts, both of you, of all thoughts except a will to make this succeed." Ambrose snored. "Sleep, poor boy," said the Vicar, "and wake rid of this incubus."

"Succubus," said Crowther-Mason.

"Come, come," rapped the Vicar. He sprinkled holy water all about, made the sign of the Cross, and then began to read aloud in a monotone:"*Exorciso te, immundissime spiritus, omnis incursio adversarii, omne phantasma, omnis legio, hominum divomque voluptas, alma Venus, caeli subter labentia signa quae mare navigerum, quae terras frugiferentis concelebras. . .*"

Crowther-Mason creased his face in astonishment, in incredulity. "Whatever are you saying, Vicar?" he asked. The candles flickered, the shadows were vast and opulent.

"Really, Crowther-Mason," said the Vicar, irritated. "This is hardly the time to give you a translation." He prepared to continue his reading aloud.

"I don't want a translation," said Crowther-Mason. "I've done some classics. Enough, anyway, to know that what you said then sounded curiously familiar."

"What of it?" almost shouted the Vicar. "Really, sir, this is unlike you. We're engaged in a matter of life or death. Please leave what you have to say till afterwards." He resumed his monotone. *"Per te quoniam genus omne animantum concipitur visitque exortum lumina solis. Te, dea, te fugiunt venti . . ."*

"There you go again," said Crowther-Mason, excited. "Are you sure you've got the right book? 'Thee, O Goddess,' you said. *'Te, dea,* something something.' "

"Are you bewitched, sir?" cried the Vicar. "This is the *Rituale Romanum.* The devil's working on you, making you mishear. What you quoted then was from Lucretius, surely. The words are not these. That's quite certain."

"That's it, that's it," said Crowther-Mason, almost leaping. "Lucretius, that's it. That's what you were reading—the opening prayer to Venus." The Vicar opened his mouth as if to swallow an apple whole. He dropped the book like a hot potato. "It's you who are being bewitched," cried Crowther-Mason. "Something's putting the wrong words in your mouth."

The Vicar picked up his book again, dusting it on his trouser-seat. "I stand for the Church," he rang out. "The whole weight of her authority stands behind me. Cleanse your heart, sir. Don't listen to those voices. Evil is abroad tonight, but good shall prevail. Let me continue."

Ambrose was seen to writhe in his sleep. "Light,

89

light," he called faintly. In immediate obedience the lights came on.

"A good omen," said the Vicar. "Now, Crowther-Mason." He breathed deeply. "There are words on this page," he said, tapping the book. "My eyes take in those words. At the cerebral junction sight changes to sound. Sound steams out to speech and meaning. There will be no derailment. Listen again." And, in great confidence, he intoned what he believed to be the words of the *Rituale Romanum: "Te nubila caeli adventumque tuum, tibi suavis dedala tellus summittit flores, tibi rident aequora ponti . . ."*

Crowther-Mason shook his head vigorously. "It's no good, no good, I tell you," he told him. "It's coming out all wrong. The station's jammed. An alien signal's coming through. Submit. She's got you just as she's got Ambrose."

"Never!" cried the Vicar. But he looked very old and unsure in the harsh light of the electrolier. He sniffed. The scent of the sea still roared through the room. "Oh, why does nothing happen?" he said pettishly. "I'm doing my best, aren't I, O God? But that effluvium still lies over everything, like a layer of dust. I feel," he said, almost talking to himself, or to a private deity inside himself, "as if I'm winding up a watch with a broken spring, or tuning in on a set when the current is cut. There's something missing. Doubts, doubts. It's easy not to doubt on the Vicarage lawn, or when facing the confirmation class. But now, when the operation faces me, the first operation—and through none of my fault, O God —when I make the incision and find the organ not where the text-books say it is, when I'm out of the dissecting-room and feel the artery warm and pulsing and horribly alive, it's all different. O give me strength,

90

strength. Now is no time for doubting. Let me try again."
But, as he was about to try again, Sir Benjamin came in, carrying a roll of fuse-wire.

"I fixed that fuse," said Sir Benjamin, happily. "No need for these candles any more." He went round blowing them out. "A queer business altogether. Somebody's been having a bit of a joke. The box was open and all the fuse-holders scattered all over the shop. Burglars, that's what I thought at first. But there doesn't seem to be anything missing." He looked, puzzled, at the Vicar's apparatus of exorcism. Then he sniffed. "Ah. Still there, I see. You trying to get rid of her, eh, Vicar? Well, carry on, carry on. Not," he said, scratching his grey old head, "that she's really much trouble, is she? A Goddess, eh? There aren't many houses round here that can boast about having a goddess. Old Foulkes is always going on about his family ghost, but he's got nothing like this. Eh? Still, if you want to, carry on, carry on." And he sat down, humming.

The Vicar was shocked. "Indifference," he said. "That's the trouble with this parish. Nobody's on any side. But don't you see, Sir Benjamin, not being on any side means being on the devil's side. I'm surprised at you, a sidesman, a model to the village, a pillar of the Church. If the devil walked in here, with a clumsy shoe and his hair brushed over his horns, offering no reflection to the mirror and no shadow to the sun, what would you do? Would you make him welcome, give him whisky, discuss the crops and cricket? Surely, surely, you recognise evil?" He trembled on the last word.

"One's got to be polite in my position, you know," said Sir Benjamin. "I take people as I find them. You can't afford to make too many enemies, not at my time of life."

91

Ambrose snored.

"And you, Crowther-Mason," cried the Vicar. "Are you with me or against me? Am I fighting on my own?"

"I'm with you, Vicar," said Crowther-Mason reasonably, "but do I have to accept your premises? We have to free Ambrose of this incubus or succubus, but how can we be sure your technique is the right one? How can you be sure she's evil?"

"Really. . . ."

"No, no, wait. I've never thought of her as evil, and if I haven't that's partly the fault of my Christian education. We're two-faced, the lot of us, in our attitude to the classics. We're taught to bow down before Homer. We're told to accept Virgil as an honorary Christian. And all the time we're asked to regard the myths they wrote about, the myths that are the very blood of their work, as mere fairy stories. But myths are *not* fairy stories. Our smug little hymns are too ready to suffer a key-change. The equivocal engine's too well oiled. This won't do at all. We can't have it both ways. We must think of some other way, we must invoke other authorities. If she's alive, surely the others must be, her Olympian colleagues, I mean. Someone must be responsible for her."

The Vicar shuddered. "This is monstrous," he said. "You're suggesting we treat with the devil, bargain with the enemy. No! The Church had the power at the first to drive them screaming underground, branded and seared with the scorching iron of the Cross. That power remains, and I, though all unworthy, am a minister of that power. Very well, I shall wrap the cloak of my faith about me and venture into the storm alone." He sighed. "May I drive out not only this evil but also your incapacity to see evil." He picked up his book again, leafed it through to the right page, and resumed. *"Adiuro ergo te, draco nequissime, in nomine Agni immaculati . . ."* Sir Benjamin and Crowther-Mason waited patiently but sceptically. Ambrose snored quite happily.

9

". . . *QUI ambulavit super aspidem et basiliscum, qui conculavit leonem et draconem, ut discedas. Discede. contremisce et effuge!*" But the words didn't sound like a command, they sounded like a desperate plea, one that no self-respecting spirit could be expected to do more than laugh at. The Vicar sweated (it was very warm and seemed to be growing warmer), Ambrose still snored, Crowther-Mason kept looking at his watch and yawning covertly, Sir Benjamin drank a bottle of hock and ate some thick clumsy turkey sandwiches he had made for himself in the kitchen. Munching, Sir Benjamin said:

"She doesn't seem to have gone. That smell's still there, stronger than ever in fact. There's nothing like sea air to give you an appetite." And, contentedly, he tucked into a slab of white meat ill-hid by its bread carapace and plastron.

"I make that just an hour," said Crowther-Mason. "An hour of holy water and Latin."

"Failed," groaned the Vicar, desperate-eyed. "And yet it can't be the Church that's failed. It's I who've failed, I, I. There must be a hole in the tooth undiscoverable by the dentist's mirror. The vessel isn't clean. But why isn't it clean? I've scoured it, polished it. I'm unworthy. But how, how, how can I be made worthier?" Like any Old Testament patriarch visited by plagues and boils, he tore at his grey hair, saying, like the dying Falstaff, "God God God."

"You must," said Crowther-Mason kindly but firmly, "open your eyes to a shocking heresy. Shocking because it's true. A new religion, as I see it, is not concerned with merely superseding the old but with enclosing it as well. Enclosing it. Containing it." His hands made enclosing, containing gestures. "Truth, I should think, is not a matter of slow distillation but a cumulative revelation, weaving wider circles—" he wove them "—rejecting nothing that's good, folding more and more beneath ever-widening wings. Good, however limited, can never be washed away by a greater good. Good can't cast out good. We talk about washing down bread and cheese with beer, but that isn't really so. The cheese becomes more alive, more significant, in that palatal consummation, sanctified, as it were, with a glowing halo of hops and barley." He sucked in a sudden flow of saliva. "If you see what I mean."

"We've got a fair choice of cheeses," said Sir Benjamin. He finished off his last turkey sandwich. "Double Gloucester. Stilton. Lancashire. Wensleydale. There's no country in the world for cheeses like England. Just as there's no country in the world for bread like France." He ended the hock. "That's what we'll have next," he said hungrily. "A bit of bread and cheese. Good."

"The past, you see," said Crowther-Mason, "is never discarded. The past is made richer by the unfolding present. The gods are still alive, aspects of the

"A bit of bread and cheese. Good."

breathtaking, growing, moving, widening, unifying pattern."

"No!" cried the Vicar, as if Crowther-Mason's words were thumbscrews. "No, I tell you, no! What have we Christians to do with that? A dirty spawning pantheon," he whimpered, "limping dreams of fallible minds, gods lusting like men because they were made by men. . . ."

"Everything's made by men," said Crowther-Mason. "We've got to admit it. The objective and the eternal are alike in that they're separable from the observer. But, whenever I look at a table, I *make* a table, just by the act of seeing it. The eternal isn't any less eternal because a fallible mind conceives it. Divine revelation has to end up in the mind of a human receiver. In that sense we make our gods."

The Vicar groaned. Sir Benjamin said, in wonder, "I've never heard such rot in all my born days. Is that the kind of talk you give to your constituents? No wonder we're heading for total collapse. I didn't understand one word."

"I'm not sure that I understood very much more," said Crowther-Mason. "But how can I make the Vicar feel, as I feel, that there's nothing malicious about this visitation? Why can't a goddess of love be a tangible aspect of the terrible, unknowable deity? Her personality, certainly, is rather more attractive than, say, that of St Paul. I don't see why she shouldn't be canonised, now I come to think of it. Saint Venus."

The Vicar's groans turned to an articulate mumble. He sat on the edge of an armchair, his joined hands plunged between his knees as though ready to dive into the sea-green carpet. "I've never been so embarrassed," he said. "And, to my shame, embarrassment comes before horror at blasphemy so soberly uttered, and I think,

Crowther-Mason, that you're sober. What," he said, "has the Church been to most of us, even me? A suit kept clean for ceremonial occasions. Part of the gentle English pattern, where the winter, in retrospect, has never been really so rough, the summer never a fire. The whole land's a sort of drawing-room furnished in taste, covered in pink cretonne. God, we liked to think, presided genially over the cricket club and the darts tournament. But the dust could never be disturbed, and the ancient lawn must never be mined by moles. The comforting shibboleths were enough—the simple magic of baptism, syrup for the sick, and the noble stock responses of the prayers for the dead." He got up from his chair, visibly agitated. "But now," he said, "now we travel to a fiery land where the beasts have talons and the birds secrete venom. What can I do now? I approached this problem bubbling like a child with a show-off hobby. My gun was a toy gun: it could never really frighten a burglar. Well, the burglars are in. And I tremble, impotent, at the top of the stair. There are two ways," he said, "two ways to take, but they're both unfamiliar, too unfamiliar for an old man who has no maps and knows only a lane leafy in summer, with the bells heard in the distance, and the gargoyles waiting, ready to grin a greeting for me to grin back to with a sort of love." It was becoming really a very warm night. There was a far-off play of lightning. Thunder bumbled, far off. "But," said the Vicar, putting his shoulders back as on parade, holding his head high, "let it not be said that an old man lacks courage."

"Whatever it is you propose to do," pleaded Crowther-Mason, "please don't do it. Please."

"Let the bishop stop sipping port in his sumptuous palace," declaimed the Vicar. "Let the dean pause at the ruridecanal conference. Let the curate take his eye off the ball for a moment, and look at me now." He invited the whole world to look at him, his arms spread out. "Forty years in the Church," he said. "The Church," he repeated, "the morganatic gift of a syphilitic monarch. Look at me, too old and too weak for the waterless trek in the desert, the sweating mass in the jungle, the care of the poor in the scorpion-crawling abbey. But," he said stoutly, "not too old for the renunciation of everything that meant everything." And he started to tear off his clerical collar. Sir Benjamin was shocked, saying:

"Not in my house, Vicar. Not that."

"I am not worthy," cried the Vicar. "*Domine, non sum dignus.*" He was having some difficulty with the back stud. The lightning crawled raggedly nearer, followed punctually by drums. Crowther-Mason tried to grab the Vicar's tearing hands, saying urgently, "Pull yourself together. God knows it isn't my place to say this to you, but even the saints, even the apostles knew failure. The devil's a hard nut: one's teeth fail sometimes, but the hammer may well be patience. Sometimes prayer, fasting, retreat, delirious vigil, repetition—endless repetition—of the proper ceremonies have been necessary to complete the work. God knows I, as a politician, am not much of a Christian, but if the Church gives up what's left for us? Only the mystique of Mother's Day and the ice-box or the rubber truncheon of the collective state. Don't give up, for God's sake."

"It's for God's sake I'm giving up," shouted the Vicar. "You fool, don't you realise this is only a battle of flowers? Our glorious tradition of compromise sold me to the enemy before I was born. My place should be on the justice's bench, dispensing moderate fines to the moderate law-breakers. I'm doubting this misty English Church, incapable of anything but a sort of masque of good and evil. The gargoyles are crawling down," he said, his face mad, "sharp and distinct as in Mediterranean sun, that were formerly blurred into Hallowmas bogies, and every single one has become a Medusa, and the appropriate weapons are not on the inventory. They'll turn me into stone unless I throw off the Perseus disguise and become a harmless spectator." He struggled with Crowther-Mason, and now Sir Benjamin joined the scrimmage, both the laymen trying to force him to keep his collar on. An undignified and rather grotesque struggle, while Ambrose still snored. With a triumphant rip the Vicar pulled away from his neck his badge of religious authority. He threw it wildly. "There," he cried, "there let it lie. And for the rest, let God have his will of me."

The lightning was on top of them. It flash-bulbed the garden, showing a photograph of gods unperturbed, showing also an elm struck, an elm on momentary fire, toppling. Thunder rang round the sky, almost hiding the noise of the falling tree and the noise of the falling of the thing or things it fell on. The Vicar shouted, "Evil's abroad!" in a kind of triumph, as though he were on the side of evil. "But now," he added, "we know we're naked."

"Lightning's struck," thundered Sir Benjamin. "This is no joke. Vicar, I wish, with all due respect for your cloth, that you'd reserve religion for Sunday and your own pulpit. Religion's all right in its place, but when it provokes acts of God, my sense of humour deserts me. Come on," he said to Crowther-Mason. "Let's know the worst, let's know the worst." And he thundered out. Rain immediately hissed into life, tropically pelting. But the air did not seem to grow any cooler. Crowther-Mason, putting his jacket-collar up, followed Sir Benjamin.

"Oh," groaned a voice. "Oh oh oh oh." Ambrose was coming awake. He opened bleared eyes, tried to chew his mouth, saying, "Dreaming. I was dreaming. God, I feel dry. I was dreaming that somebody was falling out of bed. Someone's been making me eat brass filings. I dreamt about that, too. Have you been fighting, Vicar, or something? And in this dream the falling out of bed was somehow tied up with the end of the world. Oh." He put out his tongue like a hanged man.

Humbly the Vicar said, "I can't tell you anything. I've nothing to report. Except that I've been dreaming, too. I was dreaming that I was awake. And the taste in my morning mouth is the taste of myself, and that's not very palatable, but it used to be my favourite dish."

"When I fell asleep," said Ambrose, "I seem to remember that you were doing something that was rather important, but I can't recall precisely what it was."

"Think," said the Vicar, nodding. "You'll remember what it was. You'll have to call in another doctor, some suave granite Jesuit who plays no cricket, or a Buddhist monk, or a painted medicine man. You're still enchanted. The evil arms are still around you, and I cannot loosen their grip."

"Oh," said Ambrose, speeding into full wakefulness. "That. So it wasn't a dream. It's cold prose. Hangover newsprint." He chewed his mouth again and then looked out sadly at the downpour. "I think," he said, "I could drink all that." He began to get up from his chair, creaking and moaning like an old man. Sir Benjamin came in, soaked and raving, followed by a soaked but not raving Crowther-Mason. "I can't go out there,

101

though," said Ambrose. "I daren't go into the dark, dare I?"

"Go where the hell you like," roared Sir Benjamin. "At least three of them smashed, smashed to atoms. An obscene mess of limbs. I hope," he roared dangerously at the Vicar, "your over-possessive butcher-god is satisfied. I know they were only statues, an old man's toys, but what have we, any of us, except toys? What has He got except toys? But He, of course, must have the nursery to Himself, spread out His bricks and let His railway monopolise the floor. We're allowed to finger His last year's annuals or work out a jigsaw with the key pieces missing. And," he cried, "we've got to be grateful if He doesn't kick us. Go and look," he ordered the Vicar. "It's all your fault, you and your blasphemy. I've a damned good mind to claim from the Ecclesiastical Commissioners."

"Easy, easy, Sir Benjamin," said the Vicar. "Be calm, man, be calm."

"I should think," said Crowther-Mason, "that it might be possible to stick them together again. Jupiter's in a pretty bad way and Neptune's headless and his trident's become Morton's fork. As for poor Venus...."

"Dead!" cried Sir Benjamin in anguish. "Smashed! Poor girl, poor, poor girl. Nothing left of her at all."

Lady Drayton came in, anxious, her hair in curlers and a rather old dressing-gown wrapped around her. "Whatever has happened?" she said. "A noise woke me up. I knew it wasn't you, Ben, coming to bed. It was much too loud for that."

Crowther-Mason explained. "Some of Sir Benjamin's statues have been sent to the stonebreaker's yard. To be quite honest, I have a feeling that they're not really stone. Some kind of clay perhaps. They gave in too

102

Lady Drayton came in.

103

easily. A tree," he explained further, "was struck by lightning."

"His fault." Sir Benjamin pointed at the Vicar. "He brought it on with his blaspheming."

"Vicar," said Lady Drayton, "whatever have you been doing to yourself?" He looked like an intellectual tramp, one, perhaps, who had been forced to take to the road because of pederasty.

"I ..." said the Vicar. "You see ..." He began peering on to the floor, looking for his collar. He then went down on all fours, searching, making bear-like noises.

"Is everybody mad tonight?" asked Lady Drayton. "And what's that light up there?" The rain was easing. There could be seen very clearly a sort of celestial spotlight, greenish-blue.

"A satellite," said Crowther-Mason. "The Americans or the Russians, I'm not sure which. I don't suppose it matters which, really."

"This is the end," said Sir Benjamin, bunched up in a chair, while the Vicar was still on all fours, "the end of something in me. The end of sun and sea and vineyard, and the beginning of the victorious north. The past is dead, and the unblinking arc-light of the eternal present takes over."

"Oh, nonsense," said Lady Drayton briskly. "It shouldn't take long to clear up the mess. We might even start a rockery."

10

THE RAIN stopped and the sky cleared. Like some travelling hangman the lightning passed on to another county. Sir Benjamin was easily persuaded to go and cut himself collops of bread and cheese to eat with a whole raw onion or two. Lady Drayton became aware of perturbation among the servants. Spatchcock was talking fearfully about divine judgments and the cook was on her knees. Of Diana's old nanny there was nothing to be seen. And Sir Benjamin's twin brother, bedded snug with his duodene of whisky, seemed to sleep through everything. Lady Drayton went to quieten the noise of the servants, saying, "There, there."

Ambrose, Crowther-Mason and the Vicar (who had found, but not yet donned, his collar) became conscious almost simultaneously of a change in the atmosphere of the drawing-room.

"It's gone!" cried Ambrose. "Or am I starting a cold?"

"Yes," said Crowther-Mason. "It's gone. The tide's out. Or we've exchanged Brighton for Southport. The smell of the sea has completely disappeared."

"It's worked," said Ambrose. "Your spell *has* worked. I am now disenchanted. God help me," he added.

The Vicar gasped. "What do you mean?"

"It's true," exulted the Vicar. "The heavy, brooding, obsessive presence has lifted." And it was true, too. The night smelt of night-scented stock, wet grass and earth, lightning-blasted leaves. "The devil has crawled off," said the Vicar, "to his noisome pit. God be praised. How could I doubt again? I was too impatient." And, impatiently, he tried to fix his collar back on.

"Of course, of course," said Crowther-Mason, pounding his left palm with his right fist. "I was a fool. This was bound to happen. Vicar, I'm afraid that it wasn't your little ceremony that did the trick. It was the lightning. God, or Theos, or Deus, or x, or whatever you like to call Him always knows what He's doing."

The Vicar gasped. "What do you mean?"

"Man always knows the answer," said Crowther-Mason, "but always refuses to act on it. If only Sir Benjamin had let us remove that ring with a hammer-stroke, this whole night's business would never have happened. Now Thor or Jove or Jehovah has, in his wholesale massacre, destroyed the bond which led to poor Ambrose's anticipating his honeymoon in a way he hadn't foreseen. That finger, certainly, no longer holds a ring. I should have realised all this before, fool that I am. I actually saw fingers in the grass. The ring I didn't see. The ring flew off, I suppose. Anyway, Ambrose is free."

"But," protested the Vicar, "it was my act of exorcism. If I hadn't failed, I wouldn't have doubted. If I hadn't doubted I wouldn't have blasphemed. If I hadn't blasphemed that expression of divine anger would never have shot home to that elm-tree."

"What are you after all?" said Crowther-Mason. "Only a man. A man without a collar." The Vicar tried again. The stud seemed to be lost. "You'll never know the answer," said Crowther-Mason. "Trees are often struck by lightning. We'll none of us ever know. Stick to theology. I'll stick to politics. Ambrose will return to structural engineering. God is what He is."

"Free, you said," said Ambrose with sudden anger. "I'm free. Free for what? Free to be what I was. A dimension's been removed. It's as though, while savouring the exhilarating three-dimensional world, one were suddenly enchanted into a film. Now I'm just canvas. Or cardboard. Flat, monochrome. I was lifted above the mechanical roundabout of time," he said sadly, "sucked out of the stream of history, raised by her to the timeless level of a myth. Adonis is dead now. Death is just another name for the state of being myself. Ambrose Rutterkin, the moderately successful engineer, whose school career was not particularly distinguished, who is quite well-liked because he stands his corner and always agrees with what people say. What have I now to give me uniqueness? I'm the man on the tube-train going to work in the morning, indistinguishable from the rest of the drove, fussy about small things but with no real convictions. Reality seems to have departed. I may as well resume the ordinary mask which will always be my face from now on; borrow a toothbrush and a suit of pyjamas from Jack here; wind up the alarm-clock to remind me that time is real; prepare for what they call life. There's another bed in your room, isn't there, Jack?" said Ambrose.

"There is. But why?"

"I'll go to it now. Tomorrow, if, as you say, my car's been struck by lightning, I've an early train to catch."

"Not struck by lightning," said Crowther-Mason patiently. "Your car is in a ditch. You can ring up the garage now if you like. Or I will. It's your bride that was, indirectly, struck by lightning."

"First thing in the morning," said Ambrose tiredly. "I'll ring up then. It's been a long day. It's been a long night. And, Vicar," he said, "I suppose I ought to say thank you." He smiled bitterly. "Thank you." He went out, dragging his feet. He turned at the door. "I'm wearing pyjamas," he said. "I don't need to borrow any. Thanks all the same." He could then be heard mounting the stairs wearily.

"Nobody ever said anything about pyjamas," said the Vicar. "Poor lad." He sighed very deeply. "I seriously think, Crowther-Mason, that I ought to retire. I ought to resign my living and burn my mouldering library and then go and vegetate on the South Coast. Things have come alive too late for me. I can almost see tomorrow, with its nuptial duties, as the final flowery night of the run of a popular play."

"Heavens, I'd almost forgotten," said Crowther-Mason, starting. "Tomorrow is the real problem, a wall to be scaled that hides the rest of the assault course. Everything else is tucked away in the ragbag drawer of the future. Surely you've heard that Diana refuses to marry? Didn't you catch Ambrose's closing words? He accepts the situation. He's going away in the morning."

"I don't take this seriously," said the Vicar, his old self, shaking his head. "Many a young couple look forward to marriage when the frail barricade of time still looks solid. Then, when it starts to melt, their courage melts with it. But, when it's actually melted—the wall, I mean, holding the event off from them—well, the only thing to face is the event itself. That's really solid and so less frightening than a crumbling wall. This sort of thing's always happening. There's no problem that night won't dispel. The bride may cry at the altar and the bridegroom may tremble, anticipating the bed ready made in the seaside hotel, but they'll go through with it. I've brought many a marriage into the world and always had a safe delivery."

Lady Drayton came back, her husband accompanying her. He had in one hand a terrifying hunk of bread and cheese, in the other a raw onion. He munched at these alternately, weeping copiously but alert again, no longer self-pitying. "Well, Vicar," said Lady Drayton, "you must think me a poor hostess, and as for my husband . . ."

"He was very welcome," said Sir Benjamin indistinctly. Onion-tears flowed richly. "Welcome to anything we've got." He sniffed. "It's gone," he said. "Did I imagine it? The sea's receded. Now it's back—" he sniffed again "—to its old smells. Furniture polish. Potted palms. Old sandwiches. Onions." He looked down at his onion-holding hand, confused. "I beg your pardon," he said, for some reason.

"The unwelcome guest has departed," beamed the Vicar. "The cloud has lifted. The devil has packed his bags and caught a train to a distant destination."

Lady Drayton frowned, puzzled. She was about to say, "Your brother, Ben?" when her daughter walked into the room by way of the French-windows. Diana, waif-like, wet, tired. "Diana!" said Lady Drayton, glad but surprised.

"Hallo," said Diana. Sir Benjamin chewed, nodding at her. She sat down, looking tiny and bedraggled. The Vicar, however, said:

"You're looking very well, my dear, very well. I'm so glad that this rumour of your illness was without foundation. I see you've been taking a moonlight walk.

Excellent, excellent. You're a little wet, I see, but you've missed all the trouble."

"Rumours are often half-right," said Diana, in a little voice. "I have been ill, in a way, but I think I've recovered. The moonlight walk was really a moonlight flitting, but I think I can pay the rent now. As for trouble, I've had my own share of that. Do you mind if I talk to mother?"

"You'd better come upstairs," said Lady Drayton, "and get dry. Your hair's soaked. And look at the state of your clothes."

"I'm an intruder," said the Vicar. "I was just going anyway. God bless you, my dear. Good night, everybody. I look forward to seeing you all tomorrow. Oh, my case and my book and my candles. I mustn't forget those, must I?" He fussily packed up his exorcisation instruments.

"I must go and see Ambrose," said Crowther-Mason. "He must make new arrangements. His sleep must be broken by another thunderbolt. This time, I think, one as feathery as a dream. He can wake from a dream to a dream."

Sir Benjamin went on with his bread and cheese and onion, weeping like a bride.

11

LADY DRAYTON sat on the single bed in her daughter's bedroom, watching while Diana dried her hair in a bath-towel, clad in a Chinese dressing-gown that was all dragons. On the walls were some of her paintings—juvenilia, she now loftily called them: a limping lopsided circus group, not so good as Picasso; a cane-bottomed chair after Van Gogh; a still-life of newspapers, wine-bottles, oranges that all seemed twisted and crying out with a sort of still pain; flowers of impossible colour. "They were all going on," said Lady Drayton, "about ozone and draughts of fishes in the drawing-room and about witchcraft and what they were going to do about it. I was the female equivalent of dog-tired and your father would keep shaking me and telling me to come down and be thoroughly frightened. I just wanted to lie in bed and worry in peace."

"I'm sorry," said Diana. "I've been bad."

"If I had my time over again," said Lady Drayton, "I'd think twice about having an only child. It's my own fault, I suppose, spoiling you as I have. You've had your own way once too often. I think even you realise that."

"This is the last time." Diana began to brush her hair.

"It was my own fault," said Lady Drayton, "encouraging a sort of sisterly affection for Ambrose, turning him into a sort of ready-made visiting brother. The brother is never the boss. This was bound to happen. In some ways it was hard to fight that Julia of yours. You need a strong hand over you, but not that sort of strong hand. Were you so thoroughly blind as not to see what she was?"

"I think I knew," said Diana, "but it didn't seem to matter."

"It seems to matter now."

"I suppose it does. If you want a masculine principle you should seek it in a masculine body, or at least a male one. Small things will topple an edifice," said Diana. "The tiniest pressure will kill, if you know where to apply it. It was a small thing that happened tonight."

"You still haven't told me what happened tonight," said Lady Drayton. "How you got your clothes in such a state."

"I'm telling you now," said Diana, sitting down in the one armchair of the bedroom. She smelt pleasantly of damp clean hair. "Something quite commonplace happened. We hadn't got very far down the London road when we had a puncture. Now I come to think of it, the cause of the puncture was rather extraordinary. There was a sort of dart lodged in the tyre, not quite a dart either, a sort of arrow. Anyway, that's not important. We had to change the tyre, obviously. Julia got to work, or tried to, and, do you know, it was really pitiful. The self-sufficient masculine shell seemed to melt like wax. She became as good an example of helpless,

113

palpitating femininity as I've ever seen. She just didn't seem to know how to do anything with her hands. Then I thought about Ambrose. I know he's an engineer and it's hardly fair to make these comparisons. But, stranded on the road as we were, without another car in sight, the night closed round me like a prison and then opened up into a desert. And suddenly I wanted somebody's strength, and I thought of Ambrose. I seemed to see him tonight for the first time. I saw him as a man, a mountain principle, and Julia had liquefied into a stream. I ran away in a kind of hysteria till I couldn't hear Julia's voice calling me back. Then the thunder and lightning were on top of me and the rain started. Still I ran, and I could hear Julia trying to run after me. But she can't run. She's a whisky-drinker and she smokes too much. She was panting after me, but she soon had to give up the chase. Abstract Julia from the carpeted, sodium-lighted world which is hers, and she becomes really pathetic. That's what I felt then. That's what I feel now. Anyway, I got off the London road and just kept on walking. Soon I was able to thumb a lift. A lorry stopped and brought me as far as the village. Then I walked the rest of the way."

"If I've told you once," said Lady Drayton, "I've told you a thousand times, never accept a lift from a strange man. You never know what might happen to you."

"The driver was rather sweet," said Diana, "and *very* intellectual. He talked about André Gide and Marcel Proust. He'd been, so he told me, a schoolmaster, but was now trying to better himself."

"Anyway," sighed Lady Drayton, "you're home, and someone ought to be thanked for it. Your father was really worried about the tons of food that wouldn't be eaten, and all the wine. He doubted his ability to get through the lot himself. And then there was the prospect of sending all the presents back. Dear, dear, dear."

"Well." Diana looked tired and not particularly happy. "The spring's been wound up," she said, "only to be released again. The sleeping relatives and the press photographers can rest assured that tomorrow will bring what they expect: bells, bouquets and all the rest of it. And for me the future, in the shape of an unknown bed in an unknown hotel, is waiting to emerge. The big gun has misfired. I feel a little deflated."

"You're just like your father," said Lady Drayton. "You live in a room full of mirrors. You may have forgotten it takes two to make a marriage. Ambrose might like to know you've come back."

"Jack's gone to see Ambrose. It seems he's sleeping here tonight for some reason." She began to look sharp and vengeful. "I've one or two things to tell him. His flying cerebrum, fuelled by brandy, should be grounded by now. He was thoroughly drunk tonight, disgustingly drunk. He said some things—or rather the spirituous speaker who hired his hall said some things he may have forgotten. But I shall remind him. Oh, yes. He's not going to be allowed to think that I've crawled back to him, the submissive little woman awed by a larger larynx. Oh, no."

"For heaven's sake," pleaded Lady Drayton, "don't start a row. There'll be time enough: you've all your lives in front of you. Let your grievances mature, lay down a cellar of wrongs—real and imaginary—for future decanting. Then you'll never be short of something to beguile the long winter evenings. Meanwhile it's early summer and, having given the sap a chance to rise, it's only fair to let the honey start flowing. There'll be time enough, as I say, time for sourness, when milk follows the honey."

"I'm almost a wife," said Diana. "And a wife's first duty is to teach her husband his place. Stern daughter of the voice of God. Duty calls."

"Have it your own way." Lady Drayton yawned. "What a child I've reared. I can't say I envy Ambrose. Still, he's a man, and men feel differently about women from women. Now I'm going to bed. Good night and God bless you. Don't stay up too late with Ambrose, and don't be too hard on each other. Marriage is the only job that begins with a holiday. It's the only one you'll get and, believe me, you'll need it."

Diana kissed her mother. "Good night, Mummy," she said. ' Thank you for everything, especially for being my mother." The pictures on the walls seemed to wince at that.

"I've fulfilled my biological function," said Lady Drayton, "and I always felt it would be nice for someone to thank me for it. I suppose I'd better go before you're betrayed into further sentimentality." And she went. Diana smiled, made up her face complacently, tied her hair in a ribbon, opened her door, found the corridor empty, then went downstairs to the drawing-room. She poured herself a small glass of whisky and helped herself to a cigarette. She was looking forward to a short sharp session of rebuking Ambrose. She sat in an arm-chair, her back to the door, her face to the French-window. The moon had risen. Jack Crowther-Mason had promised to send Ambrose down here to see her. With a nasty smile she heard entering male feet, a male cough.

"Well, Ambrose," she said, "I trust you've slept it off."

"It's not Ambrose," said Crowther-Mason. "And

as for sleeping it off, that depends what you mean."

Diana turned, annoyed. "Jack!" she recognised. "Where *is* Ambrose?"

"He's sitting up in bed," said Crowther-Mason. "He's smoking. The verb is transitive but it suggests, I hope, a hotter temperament than ever seemed possible to Namby Pamby of the Lower Fourth."

"So," said grim Diana, "he *hasn't* slept it off."

"As I say," said Crowther-Mason, "it all depends what you mean. He's perfectly sober, except for a slight uncertainty as to the relative locations of cigarette and mouth. But he asks me particularly to tell you that if you've come crawling back you can crawl back to where you've crawled from. Please regard me as Hansard, perfectly impersonal. I report verbatim."

"What else does he say?" asked Diana, becoming fascinated.

"He says," said Crowther-Mason, "that if you expect him to come crawling to you (the idea of crawling seems nevertheless very much in his mind, you'll notice) if you expect that, he says, you're mistaken. He says he refuses to ooze things like 'Forgive me, darling' and 'How could I be such a brute' and 'Let's kiss and make up' all over the carpet. (You'll see, nevertheless, he had those clichés in mind.) He says he knew this would happen. He also says he's quite prepared to marry you out of pity and as long as it's fully understood that this represents considerable condescension on his part. He says that he's had a very tempting offer which, in his magnanimity, he's rejected because of an altruism which, he says, nothing, not even another's egotism, would make him abandon. The wedding may proceed, as far as he's concerned, he says. Lack of consideration has never been one of his characteristics, he says, and he would hate to see so many

117

"What else does he say?" asked Diana, becoming fascinated.

disappointed. In short, he's willing to accept you as a bride *on his conditions*. Again, let me hasten to add that I'm merely a dictaphone. I refrain from editorial comment. That had better be left to you."

"You," said Diana, tight-lipped, "can leave it to me."

"Oh," said Crowther-Mason, "he finally asks me to tell you that he's graciously willing to receive you. He's prepared to grant an audience, he says, and he adds that *his* bedroom door isn't locked."

"I wish," said Diana ungrammatically, "it *was* locked. I could kick it open then. On his terms! Ambrose is going to marry me on *my* terms. It's a good thing I came back. As soon as he's free from my restraining influence, this is what happens. Drunkenness. Lechery. He thinks he can do what he likes. We'll soon change that. I hope he expects the worst. I should hate to see him disappointed." And she rushed out, dressing-gown tight about her, a pretty flushed girl, angry, full of words. Crowther-Mason laughed to see her go.

I 2

LEFT alone for the first time for several hours, Crowther-Mason became aware of unwonted feelings in himself. He felt a strange desire for luxurious abandon: his glands were flushed with the most voluptuous images: his whole body seemed to be turning into some Oriental or Silver Latin book on amation. He smiled quizzically with surprise at this. At the same time he seemed to see that love—impersonal, undifferentiated—was possible to all men. This was astonishing. Looking out from the French-windows on the summer night, looking up, he observed that the green-blue light in the sky was pouring on to the earth, with a sort of urgency, a kind of liquid benevolence. He wondered if that was really an earth satellite. There had been so many lately: the Russians and the Americans vying with each other as young boys vie with each other, arching higher and higher, in school urinals. But surely no rays of benevolence would pulse out of such a heavenly body! Crowther-Mason was, though a politician, no sentimentalist, yet it seemed to him that the whole earth tonight was bathed in what, for want of a better term, could only be called love. And the quiet summer night had ceased to be quiet: from the village came sounds, it seemed, of joy and revelry. Could that light in the sky be the planet Venus? Impossible, according to the astronomers. The next transit of Venus would not be till the year 2004. And yet Venus was obviously, after her stone death and the dissolution of her earthly marriage, intent on rising to heaven, showering warmth, odour and light on the world as a witness of the power of love. While Crowther-Mason drank in, in wonder and astonishing content, the heady vinous scents of this night, the Vicar suddenly appeared, dancing across the garden, his arms held out as for an embrace. In one hand there seemed to be a flower. Panting, he almost fell upon Crowther-Mason, crying:

"Crowther-Mason, or may I call you Jack? Away with the restricting clothes of surnames! What a night this is! I felt I had to come back to reaffirm my faith, a faith which is now so firm as to reverse all order. It was a second-hand faith that I carried all these years. Now it shines like a birthday present. Oh, to be happy! My very body is reaffirmed in the glory of its flesh, though ageing. My flesh is reformed. The blood skates through my arteries; I could digest a whole sheep; my mind seethes with inchoate poems. What a night this is!" And he danced a sort of pavane.

"I'm glad you're happy, Vicar," said Crowther-Mason. "Very glad."

"Call me Norman," cried the Vicar. 'Norman is the name my mother gave me. Have you noticed that light in the sky? Yes, yes, I see you have. But the streets in the village are flowing in gold. The very beer in the working-man's club must be singing a paean. Exotic flowers are appearing in the most unlikely places. Look at this." He held up his flower. "I found this in the church."

. . . dancing across the garden.

"A crypt orchid?" said Crowther-Mason.

"People in the streets," said the Vicar, "are dancing, kissing each other. The long-married couple who've exhausted all conversation and sit all Saturday night over taciturn stout—they are babbling with new enthusiasm. The cats are wailing in most melodious counterpoint, bitches have had a miraculous accession of heat. In the municipal zoo there must be amorous pandemonium: probosces wantonly wreathing, capillary erections of leopards and panthers. Probably even the tortoise moves with a sort of leisurely impetuosity. And the air is full of the headiest distillation, chiming madly like bells. It's like a gratuitous Christmas, an antipodeal Christmas. And even I, I feel the fire which I thought safely out, the fire which I thought sublimated to a weary smoke. Venus has risen."

"Venus has risen," nodded Crowther-Mason. "I must confess that even the cold heart of a politician has been touched. I feel somehow that with very little prompting I could embrace the Leader of the Opposition."

"I know my course now," cried the Vicar. "Tomorrow and all the succeeding tomorrows can't dawn fast enough. I shall burn all my sermons and start again. There'll be no more text-chopping, no more guarded homilies, no more guarded glances at the first premonitions of sleep in the pews of the gentry. Love is my theme, love, and I now see no reason why it should ever have been anything else. It's so simple, so obvious. One searches everywhere for a collar-stud, say, and there it is, all the time, in one's trouser turn-up. Love. *Sanctificatur nomen tuum, Venus Caelestis, per omnia saecula saeculorum.*" he sang. "And if that's blasphemy, I'm past caring, but I somehow don't think it *is* blasphemy. My past life has been the real blasphemy. I've been too analytical, too niggling, too concerned with splitting the spectrum and forgetting about the living rainbow. I could sing, but none of the hymns I know—a wilder music than the four-square dirges of Ancient and Modern, a faun-like music, full of flutes and unsubmissive to text-book harmony, full of the dreadful primal innocence."

"I can feel it," said Crowther-Mason. The sky seemed to be on fire. The song in the heavens would burst itself with its own vehemence. "The moment must be taken," he said. "This mass may never be said again: this host is raised for an hour's adoring. There's only one song, and that is a song from the waste wood of history. To-night the bibulous dustman will know it, the postman, the frowsty trull and the bookmaker's clerk will know it. It's a song that the mice squeal, that the cats, through the painful courtship, already intone. Strange how all our speech this evening has been verging on verse. We were getting ready for this." He looked at the Vicar, and the Vicar seemed transformed, almost luminous. The Vicar nodded, saying:

"I know the song." And he began to recite, in a full voice: *"Cras amet qui numquam amavit . . ."*

". . . Quique amavit cras amet," completed Crowther-Mason. And the Vicar translated:

"Tomorrow will be love for the loveless, and for the
                                        lover love.
The day of the primal marriage, the copulation
Of the irreducible particles; the day when Venus
Sprang fully-armed from the wedding blossoms of
                                        spray
And the green dance of the surge, while the flying
                                        horses

Neighed and whinnied about her, the monstrous conchs
Blasted their intolerable joy."

"Music!" cried Crowther-Mason. "Where's that music
coming from?" But he found his mouth and entire vocal
apparatus taken over by some force outside himself, saying:

"Tomorrow will be love for the loveless, and for the
                                        lover love.
The swans, with garrulous throats, crash through the
                                        pools
In a blare of brass; the girl that Tereus
Forced to his will complains endlessly
Among the poplars, desperately forcing
The heartbreak message through, but only forcing
More and more ironic sweetness till
The ear faints with excess of sweetness."

And then, like some image of ancient royalty, her old
dressing-gown like a phosphorescent robe of rare metal,
Lady Drayton glided into the room, her mouth open,
words ventriloquising out:

"Tomorrow shall be love for the loveless, and for the
                                        lover love.
The scrubbing and dusting, the worry about what to eat,
The stretched elastic of wages and housekeeping money
Ready to snap, the vertigo vista of debt
Shall no longer seem important; the housewife's fingers
Shall lose their creases of grime; the husband's hair,
Receding, will give him a look of Shakespeare. Honey
Will flow from the lips that meet in perfunctory
                                        greeting;
The good-night kiss will suddenly open a door,
And sleep then will be a banquet with lights and music."

125

Sir Benjamin appeared, still fully dressed, astonished at himself saying:

"Tomorrow shall be luck for the luckless, and for the
                                        lucky luck.
The luckless punter will have unbelievable luck
And the bookmaker doubt his vocation. Houses will
                                        echo
With a fabulous smell of frying onions, steaks
Will be featherbeds of salivating thickness.
Beer will bite like a lover and prolong its caress
Like cool arms in a hot bed. And clocks
Shall, in the headlong minute before closing-time,
Not swoop to the kill, but hover indefinitely,
Like beneficent hawks."

It was with no surprise that the four of them now saw the lovers appear, handsome and lovely, clad in moon and sun and love, Ambrose saying:

"Tomorrow shall be love for the loveless, and for the
                                        lover love."

Diana said, as out of a dream:

"The bed will be no monster's labyrinth,
But spirals winding to a blinding apex,
Sharp as a needle, where the last shred of self
Is peeled off painlessly, and space and time are bullied
Into carrying their own burdens. Tomorrow
Shall be love for the loveless. . . ."

"And," said Ambrose, "for the lover love.
The map of love, spread on our knees, disclosing
The miraculous journey, shall not terrify
With lack of compass-points, with monstrous patches
Of terra incognita. Every sea-lane

126

Leads us home to each other, and always home
Is a new continent, of inconceivable richness."

"Tomorrow," Diana began to say, "shall be love . . ."
But at that moment the light seemed to dip, the warmth
recede. Julia Webb stood at the door, taking off her
gloves, saying bitterly:

"Quando ver venit meum?
Quando fiam uti chelidon ut tacere desinam?

I got those lines," she said, in her sharp confident
manner, "from the notes to Mr Eliot's *The Waste Land*.
For the benefit of engineers and others, I translate:
'When is my spring coming? When shall I become like a
swallow and cease to be silent?' I've missed the boat,
haven't I? I've failed." Chill struck the room. The
others looked at each other, a little ashamed, as if caught
sleeping or compelled, by drink, to grotesque and unten-
able enthusiasms.

13

DIANA spoke first. "What are you doing here?" she asked. "Why did you come back?" Ambrose looked ready to hit, unspeakable thought, a woman. Sir Benjamin did not seem to remember who this woman was. Crowther-Mason turned his back on her. That light was fading, leaving the sky fast.

"I came back," said Julia Webb calmly, "because your wedding is tomorrow. You did me the honour of asking me to be your chief bridesmaid. I hope the post is still open."

"How did you get back?" asked Diana, sounding somewhat guilty.

"In my car. I waited till somebody kindly stopped to ask what the trouble was. He was a nice man, some men are. He changed my wheel very skilfully." She looked neat, crisp, well made-up, as though she had not been in a tempestuous open-air of rain, lightning and Venus.

"But I don't understand," said Diana. "After to-night, I mean. I somehow thought you'd never want to see me again. For that matter, I never thought I'd want to see you again."

"The melodramatic grand renunciation," said Julia Webb, "was never much in my line. I was never one for going out into the night, never more to be seen. I knew very well tonight what was going on in your mind. It was most unfortunate, that sudden deflation of the carefully built-up image. Like a faulty nail that precipitates the picture on to the hearth-rug. It doesn't really matter. There's plenty of time, there are plenty of disguises, plenty of other roads. But don't imagine, Diana, that I've come back crawling. . . ."

"Well-named," said Ambrose violently. "A web, that's what she is, a fly-trap. Go on, go. Get out. You're not to see Diana again. I forbid it, do you hear? Go on, get out."

Julia Webb smiled. "Don't be alarmed, Ambrose," she said. "Diana knows who she loves. The two of you are insulated from me, in one sense. In another sense, I'll always be there, like the irritant in the oyster, like a witch at a christening. The enemy, if you like. You need me, you know. I'm the gravitational pull that'll keep your marriage upright. Lady Drayton," she said, "forgive my bad manners. I've been a shocking guest. But I promise you I'll behave tomorrow."

"I suppose, really," said Diana, thoughtfully, "I couldn't bear *never* to see you again."

"It would be a frightful waste of that very lovely dress," sighed Lady Drayton. "We all make mistakes, I suppose. I've too bad a memory to indulge in recriminations." She shivered. It was almost cold. "We've a long day ahead of us," she said, "and it's very late."

"Yes, yes," said the Vicar. "How dark and cold it seems after that blaze of glory. Still, we have the memory of that light, and that candle will cheer me to bed."

"Oh, God!" said Crowther-Mason. "We're back where we started. The ring!"

"Yes, the ring," said Ambrose, aghast. "We still haven't got a ring."

"What's happened to the ring?" asked Diana with fire. "Don't say you forgot to get one!"

"Diana," said Ambrose, "the story of that ring will enliven many a winter evening. To recount it now would be intolerably tedious. But lost it is, and through nobody's fault."

"It means, then," said Crowther-Mason, "a trip to town tomorrow morning. Or else a long scrabble among the ruins."

"Ruins," said Sir Benjamin sadly, "all in ruins."

"Or, of course," said Crowther-Mason, "there's still Diana's nanny, isn't there?"

"What exactly is going on?" asked Diana.

"Now I come to think of it," said Lady Drayton, "it's strange that we've seen so little of her this evening. She's usually recounting interminable erotic sagas, washed down with cocoa, to a crowded open-mouthed kitchen. She must have gone to bed early, feeling her age at last. Strange that the strange events and the noise and the light didn't wake her. I'll knock on her door on the way to what I hope will be my final unbuckled wheel of slumber."

"Don't say things like that, Winifred," growled Sir Benjamin. "It sounded like one of those arty euphemistic epitaphs in *The Times*. I felt a chill just then. Somebody walking over my grave."

"Come on, then," said Lady Drayton. "Bed, everyone. It's going to be a long day tomorrow." So she and Julia Webb went off, Julia Webb unabashed. Sir Benjamin said to the Vicar:

"Come and have a little snack of something before you go home. Eating is the only durable pleasure left to old men, except, of course, drinking."

"Animal pleasures, Sir Ben," said the Vicar happily. "There are others, as I hope you'll see from the sermon I insist on preaching tomorrow. My new-found faith is ready to burst its bottle."

"We'll have a bottle as well," said Sir Benjamin. "And don't be too hard on animals. I've heard some dogs give uncanny imitations of human beings imitating dogs. I've heard cats cry in impeccable Cockney vowels. There's a lot of good in animals, especially when they're killed and cooked."

"Good night, my children," sang the Vicar. He left with Sir Benjamin. "Love one another," he called from without the door.

"Time enough for love when the table's cleared," rumbled Sir Benjamin.

"Well, Diana my love," said Ambrose, "I suppose I must find my way back to my lonely room where the trouble started. It means knocking the landlord up, I suppose." He smiled at her. Desire would be holy tomorrow, but tomorrow seemed a whole calendar away. He wanted the earth in its momentum to roll faster and faster down the endless mountain, to splash and drown in the river of tomorrow's sun. He wanted tomorrow to be there, the two half-creatures made one, the opposite poles given their head of attraction and join lips endlessly. Morning would carry the seeds of the night; the flowering of that night they both longed for, with all their hearts. They kissed.

"There," cackled the voice of an old crone entering in her dressing-gown. "That's the prettiest sight in the world. The kisses I've seen in my time, the kisses I've

131

"it had something tied around its neck."

tasted, of all possible flavours. If pillows and bolsters could talk," she leered. "But I'm not here to talk," she said, "but to say that I'm very sorry I can't help you in this matter of a ring. Her ladyship just told me. Well, well. Had you asked me earlier I would have been only too willing and able to oblige. But I just can't. Tonight of all nights, would you believe it, I just can't help you in any way at all. You," she said with sudden sharpness, "what do you want?" For Spatchcock the maid had just diffidently entered, saying:

"Excuse me coming in like this in my dressing-gown."

"Get on with it," said the old woman.

"I think I've got something for you, sir," said Spatchcock to Ambrose. "I was in my bedroom, you see, sir, and I heard a knock at my window, my window being on the outside of the house, you see, sir, and my bedroom being also on the ground floor. I took no notice, because I often hear knocks at my window, but I never answer them. You've got to be careful in service, you see, sir."

"Get on with it," said the old woman.

"Anyway," said Spatchcock, "I opened the window, and what do you think I found? I found a pigeon there. 'Well,' I said to myself, 'that might be one of Jack Crawshaw's.' (He's a pigeon-fancier, you see, sir, Miss.) Well, I looked at it, and, would you believe it, it had something tied round its neck."

"A message from Jack Crawshaw?" suggested Crowther-Mason.

"No, sir," said Spatchcock, "a ring. Looped through a handful of hair, like. Golden hair it was. I took it from its neck and then it flew away. Cooing it was, like anything. I put two and two together, and I thought as how it might be the one that you'd lost. So I've brought it now. I hope I done right." She took from her dressing-gown pocket a golden round.

"You've done right," said Ambrose, taking it. "Thank you very much. This is certainly the one I lost." He examined it carefully, with a sort of reverence. He handed it over to Crowther-Mason.

"And what," asked Crowther-Mason, "did you do with the loop of hair?"

"It was only hair, sir," said Spatchcock. "I threw it away. I hope I done right."

"How could you know?" sighed Crowther-Mason. "How could anybody know?" So this saint left no relic. Perhaps tomorrow fires would be lighted with First Folios; perhaps a dog would go chasing a fragment of the True Cross, thrown by its master. "Never mind," said Crowther-Mason. "Never mind."

And so it was good-night from all to all. And then bed. But, before going to bed, Spatchcock fearfully said:

"If you'd do me a small favour, Miss Diana, would you tell Sir Benjamin that them statues being broken wasn't my fault? I never went near them, Miss. Honest, I swear."

14

JUST as dawn, and dawn was very early, flushed the mess of gods in the garden, Sir Benjamin came from his bed to examine the damage in daylight. He didn't feel so well. Age seemed to be creeping up on him at last. The Rabelaisian mask he'd been wearing, the pose of the Gargantuan eater and the Pantagruelian drinker— all was becoming a little too studied. He recognised that his stomach was not what it had been. He got a slight twinge of heartburn after a quite moderate meal—say, a grilled steak or so or a brace of pheasants. He couldn't hold the amount of liquor he once had been able to. Three bottles of Burgundy left him muddled and some-times rather quarrelsome.

The future, he kept thinking. The future was eating into the past, and he dreaded the future. He dreaded conquest of the past, the gods of the past, by sheer force —lightning and a fallen tree. The future appeared to him as the boorish squatting of the complacent bus-traveller, unwilling to give up his seat to a lady. The future was a twisted self-satisfied grin. He was hearing all sorts of prophecies of doom these days, and he could well believe them. The world seemed bent on smashing all its mirrors. The world was building a hall of mirrors only to see the much-multiplied image of itself shivering into fragments, the narcissistic smile turned into a distorted leer. He didn't like the prospect before him one little bit. Tomorrow's—today's—newspapers would be full of earthquakes, crop failures, rained-off cricket matches, flooded roads, diminishing exports, the unkillable widening grin of the pullulating East, the expanding machine of the almighty infallible state. Some newspapers would prophesy anarchy and the end of the world; others would threaten Utopia. He himself could only turn to the past, but he heard that it was already possible to change the past, bringing the past perpetually up to date, a perpetual jackal fawning on the present, a malleable witness with no qualms about perjury. He knew that the armies were on the march, the Tannoys blaring, the collective mind—tool of oligarchy—being fashioned under the anaesthetic of the catch-phrase and the mass-entertainment. The gods in the garden, for all the night's miraculous epiphany, were dead.

"Come to bed," said Lady Drayton. "It isn't time to get up yet. You're going to be very very tired later on in the day."

"Yes, my dear," said Sir Benjamin. "Yes, yes. This is already tomorrow, isn't it? And what does it bring?"

"It brings a wedding."

"Yes, yes, a beginning, not an end."

"A beginning," agreed Lady Drayton. "The start, the real start, of everybody's story—even, though you forget it sometimes, ours."

"Yes," said Sir Benjamin. "That touch of heartburn is passing. I'll show them all yet; I've still a few years of life in front of me. No," he said, suffering himself to be led back into the house, "no, my dear, I never really

forget. It's a good story, the best story, and—as you say —it's our story. And I'm extremely glad of it." But he yawned.

"You're tired," said Lady Drayton. "Come back to bed."

"I'm not tired," said Sir Benjamin. "I never felt less tired in my life. But I'll come back to bed."